THE LION

Cover art by Youness Elh

Lee Burton • MMXXIV • NL, Canada
ISBN: 978-0-9784257-0-8

www.leeburton.ca

THE LION

THE LION

Jad woke with a start. *Get up. Get up.* He knew better than to fall asleep.

Where is the lion?

Looking toward the trees, stomach fluttering, he popped up to his elbows. Late summer's thin light couldn't penetrate the darkness at the edge of the meadow, nor burn off the fog of sleep that had come over him. He rubbed his eyes, counting the flock milling about the high rock he was lying on—and his stomach sank. One of the sheep was missing. *Miu again. Always Miu.* He couldn't see her. He wondered if her being missing had woken him.

He stood as wobbly as a toddler, the bottoms of his torn pants snaked around his leg, but before he could pull down a breath he was hit in the shoulder and thumped hard back down onto the rock he'd been napping on. Pain scoured his palms.

The lion! said the shock that shot through his bones.

But no. The hit had finally knocked the sleep from him.

Sham, he knew. Probably backing up now to hit him again. He turned to look up into the sheep's cloudy, hate-filled, anvil eye. He grunted, leaned up and pushed her away by the face, *stupid sheep*, leaving a smear of blood from his skinned palms across the sheep's muzzle.

Sham was the largest of his flock. She bleated at him again, a vomitous grunt, then trotted off and butted her sister, Moff, who had been dozing quietly. Moff woke bleating with alarm, sending a ripple through the peaceful flock. The lambs nearest the edges spilled into the meadow.

Stinking Sham. Jad stood again, groggy, picking a tiny pebble out of his palm. Could he not just leave Sham for the lion? One morning was all it would take before the lion would come. Was there a way so it would only take Sham? It wasn't fair. She terrorized her sister and the younger ewes. None of the other sheep would miss her.

But Father would. And he would know he had let the beast take Sham.

Father always knew when he lied.

The rocky meadow sharpened as he rubbed sleep from his eyes. Half the night he had stayed up in the blank, starless dark, hunkered here among the rocks with his crook near at hand, watching the shifting shapes of the trees. The fire he'd lit had only blinded him, and he'd sat ten paces away, back on, tapping the edge of his knife on his sleeve to keep himself alert. The flock had remained awake watching with him, even the younger lambs, knowing the lion was out there. He had seen it in the trees just yesterday, long and rangy, scars across its ribs, alone and low to the ground.

He had to be alert for it. Watchful. That was the last thing he told himself while he'd let his eyes close. So he could be alert for later.

Sham had riled up the flock and they were milling about, making it hard for Jad to count, but a minute later he verified what he had known instinctively at a glance. One missing.

Miu. Always Miu trying to sneak away. Looking for her mother, who used to disappear sometimes herself, until one day she had never been found, just last year after lambing season. Before that, Miu had stayed glued to her side.

Shading his eyes, Jad walked all four corners of the large rock. He didn't spy blood, couldn't smell it. In the thickening afternoon, as the hottest part of the day came on, finally burning off the mist that had covered the mountainside, if there were blood out there the air would know.

Far below, in the lower hills, a thin line of smoke rose from Zua's shrine down in the village. This time of day, Methen normally waved about some stinky weeds for sacrifice.

Far beyond and below, between tendrils of mist and black spikes of trees, the vast glittering lake marking where the mountains met the plains sided the long smear of the town of Ren. Two days' trek by foot from the village when carrying a full pack of wool and meat for trade, it always looked peaceful from afar, on these rare days that the clouds cleared and the land rolled away in greens and grays to the horizon.

Today was proving extra clear. Jad could even see the vast tower of Mount Ancrus, the spear, as they called it in Ren, stabbing into the heavens, so high that traders who came through Ren called it by other names, and when traveling through lands and various nations, used its placement on the horizon as a guide. Few people had ever seen its base, but today Jad could see the snow painting its sides not far above the line of the horizon, and its needle-thin peak fading with its height even though there were no clouds. Nobody would ever see the whole of it but the gods.

His eyes returned to the line of smoke rising from the village. Probably Father with Methen making an offering of his own to Zua for good luck with prices when they made the trek to Ren in a few days. Ren's traders enjoyed cheating Zuans like it was good fun.

This was the first summer Father had trusted him to tend the flock alone, only the second time he'd be helping carry their wool and cheese to the merchants. His cousin Endo, who was younger than him by two years, had taken the rams, all five of them, including Methen's and Tate's, who had entrusted Father with their breeders, to a lower pasture not far from the village where Father could check in on him. He'd even given Endo Pusher, their dog, to make sure small, distracted Endo did what he was supposed to. That meant Jad's only company way up here was the likes of Sham, who kept trying to bang his head open. But considering Endo liked to build mud houses in the stream, and spun in circles when he peed, trying to wet everyone's feet, having Pusher to help was probably a good idea.

He'd wished he had Pusher's broad neck to hold on to last night in the darkness.

His side throbbed from lying on the ground. He wanted to lie back down and sleep, rest for another long watch. But he picked up his crook from where he'd laid it by the big stone, its center polished by the grip of his father's hands, larger, tougher, than his. Too tall for him, and heavy on the top as Father had carved it from the dense bole of a gnarled tree, he had grown to hate it. It swayed him as he walked, and caught between bushes.

Miu missing is your fault. If you don't find her soon, the lion will. If it hasn't already.

With the crook's heavy butt end he nudged the most stubborn sheep aside, stepping into the middle of their bleating, braying indignation, and there he raised the crook high.

"Look at me, you brainless turds," he said.

In one swift thrust, he brought the crook down hard enough to wedge it fast in the loose ground of the high meadow, down between two stones. "To me!" he said, for good measure. "I want you to all stay within ten paces of my crook. Nobody pokes a nose out!"

A ripple passed through the flock. Those many pairs of awful anvil eyes turned his way. The strays who had struck out on their own slowly ambled back towards him.

"Good," he said. "Ten paces. No more."

The sheep wouldn't move outside of that circle now. It was like he'd made an invisible bowl to put them in and they couldn't get out. Not even Sham the trickster.

He felt a twinge of guilt for his trick, and with it a pang of annoyance. He had shown Father this trick last summer and Father had grabbed him by the shoulders and shaken him. "Don't you ever do this again, Jad," Father had said, flicking him across the ear so that it stung. "Don't do it. It's lazy and … Zua condemns the use of such … trickery."

Jad had nodded, not understanding why Father wouldn't let him use a method that actually worked. The sheep really listened and didn't wander off. It was practically the only thing that did work.

But Father hadn't let go of his shoulders, his nostrils flaring. "Don't tell anybody about this! Not even Tez. Promise me you won't!"

He did promise. And he had kept it. Jad hadn't shown Tez, even when he really wanted to, those times Tez would talk all afternoon about how better it was to be a hunter like his father, never have the musk of sheep stink stuck on him—*Baar, baar,* Tez would yell at him, thrusting with his hips. *This is what you're really doing out here. Baar, baar…*

Herding the sheep had been so much easier before he had promised.

But Miu was his sister's favorite sheep. Father would understand him using the trick again just this once…

He stepped outside the swirling flock, not looking back. The problem now was just as big. Where to actually look for Miu? The meadow hung halfway up to the bottom of the sky. Black fuzz of forests lay below, the path back to the village leading off into the green, and nothing but hazy white peaks above him. Miu could have stumbled into any number of ravines or gullies and he'd never find her.

Well, if she could be anywhere, he figured he'd best start looking at the place where he least wanted to find her, the ravine by the river.

If Zua really were merciful, he'd find her before the lion found the flock while he was gone.

Up here on the mountainside, the sun much closer than down in the valleys, it scorched Jad's face as he trod rock to rock. Moss filled the gaps between many of the boulders, making them slick, so he stepped high and judged his footing carefully. Too easily he could trip and twist an ankle and nobody would come looking for him for days. He'd be like old Manu, his father's friend. Father had found his body a few years ago at the bend in the river not far from the village, a sheep carcass still hanging in his arms where the river had washed them up together onto the sandy shore. What was left of Manu's lips had been peeled back in a grin, as if he were lying there happily hugging the decaying sheep.

He has honored Zua in being a true shepherd to the end, Father said that night in front of Zua's shrine. *Zua will honor him, and so shall we.*

If Zua had wanted to honor him, Jad had thought, he could have given Manu legs that were the same length when he was born, and better balance. If Zua truly were merciful, he would have made Manu a smarter man who would have known to keep living down there in Ren, where his wife and family lived, and not join a small group of Zuans living in the mountains where his limp made him stumble along the sheep paths and sometimes slip into the river.

Jad was no old Manu. He had long strides for a boy of

twelve summers. Mother said if he got any taller he'd bound with the grace of a goat—faster than old Manu had ever run. *A true shepherd.* And he had to run. He couldn't leave the flock alone for long. It was only because it was Miu that he'd left his flock at all. If his sister hadn't named the small sheep like a pet, maybe he wouldn't feel such shame for letting her get lost. *Baby lamb,* she had named her, after her own name. Losing the sheep felt almost like losing his little sister.

His long, careful strides carried him across the face of the mountain. The wind battered this side overlooking the lake and the vast plains. The trees in the open stayed low, wrinkled, old men, and so in a way this side was the safer side, where a good shepherd could see far—but tall, brash, dark trees lined the hillside above him, and as Jad ran he watched their encroaching shadows in case one of them rose with teeth and crouched forward on quiet claws.

Numerous times he stopped, crouched, hand cupped over his ear to shush the wind. He wasn't alone. He could feel someone near, watching him. *Zua is honoring you,* his father had said when he had confessed he'd always had a good sense for when he was being watched. That night, they had brought an offering of honey to Zua's altar in the center of the village. To Jad it didn't feel like he was being honored, unless honor felt like ants crawling all over his neck that he couldn't bat away. His father had almost seemed angry when Jad had confided in him, so after that Jad kept his funny feelings to himself.

Birds sang in the tree line, and once the cry of a hawk far above stabbed down. The higher trees retreated near the ravine before they could pinch the rocky mountainside completely. The wind here chose to ram up the water's cut and keep this part of the hillside nearly naked. Jad brought the flock here every so often—days when the flies buzzed into his ears and nose at the same time—as the ravine was a pleasant place to escape so he could breathe.

The nearer he came to the river, the stronger the sense of a presence grew, the sense that he wasn't wanted, like he had broken into a home that wasn't his.

The wind surging, he crouched behind a big rock, shading his eyes to peer into the path behind. Cold air tingled in the spaces between his teeth. Away from the trees and able to see more of the mountain above and the world below, the sky loomed larger. He blinked, shaking his hands, his fingers numb. Something was wrong here. A storm had grown in his chest, flashes of lightning shooting his eyes side to side, his heart beating thunder in his ears. And yet he couldn't figure why. The long arrows of clouds zooming overhead made an anxious knot in his belly as he kept going toward the river's rocky crevice. As soon as he checked here, he'd go back; he couldn't leave the flock all alone for much longer. Not for one sheep, not with a lion around. Every step he took increased the risk that he'd return to a circle of guts and wool.

It was down by the edge of the ravine that he spotted a flash of white against the gray rocks. His spirits leapt. *Miu.* The thunder and the lightning was forgotten. Irritation thrust up from his feet and set him to moving. She was so close to the ledge, nose down over the edge. *Stupid sheep.* Everything he had been thinking faded as he leapt rock to rock toward her, missing the confidence his father's crook gave him to help steady over the larger, looser, tottering boulders.

Like the one that tipped back, stumbling him, clapping down against another with a heavy, hollow *clonk*. Miu heard it, and looking back at the noise, bleated and took her first step as if to run away, nose pointed precariously down over the ledge.

Stupid sheep. Stupid sheep. Stupid sheep. Stop!

"Miu!" he yelled out, knowing she was just a sheep and wouldn't heed him.

Not that his sister would either. So maybe she had named the lamb perfectly.

He was still twenty running paces away when the sheep's fat rump tipped up, spilling her over the edge.

Stupid sheep!

Head over heels, she vanished.

Jad skidded to a halt, punching the air in frustration, and shouted a swear that echoed far down in the ravine over the hush of the rushing water. What would he say to Father? What would he say to his little sister? He couldn't go after her. He thought of old Manu dragged from the river still clutching one of his sheep in his dead arms.

Then, to his astonishment, the ewe's rump appeared again, as if lifted by an invisible hand, rising back up over the ledge and wiggling clumsily back down onto the grass.

Jad hunkered into a fighting stance. *What...?*

She'd risen as if being pushed up.

Miu bleated up into the air, gently, as if content, then trotted along the edge toward a sprouting of green.

Jad watched her happily trotting along the scrubby cliffside. The sense of a presence had clamped like a hand over his mouth and nose and ears. He felt uneasy, as if he had been spoken to and had not answered.

"Who's there?" he asked, quietly first, thinking maybe there was somebody just out of sight, down over the edge of the ravine. Then louder, more bravely, disappointed in how thin his voice had sounded: "Who's there? Show me!"

Yes. It was like he heard a chorus of voices breathe the word in the clouds above and from the rocks below.

The wind slowed, rising as a hot puff in his face. The clouds zooming overhead froze. Jad turned just in time to see the mountain above him wobble. It looked like it was inching lower, lower, *Or am I falling?* Then the mountain itself, to his surprise, slid away like water.

Jad felt sick. He plonked to his knees, heaving in cool air, a bubble rising in his throat. The land had shifted while the ground beneath his feet stayed firm. He took a few more gulps before he could look up again.

The ravine, the river, the mountain, were gone. All around him spread a vast green meadow. He shut his eyes tightly, sure what he was seeing was a dream. *Too big.* No meadow, not even the plains that stretched to the east of Ren, could be so huge, and without flowers, without trees. It was flat and perfect, with bright, low grass as far as the eye could see.

Under him, the soft grass stalks tickled his sensitive, scraped palms. He opened his eyes again, distantly noting that he should be afraid. This place, it wasn't just in his imagination, he was really seeing it. Yet he felt safe here, content. The storm that had been raging in his chest settled. He no longer felt like he had been spoken to, but words sat heavily in his throat like there was something he was supposed to say.

Ten paces from him stood a man at least twice as tall as him—and Jad was tall for his age, one of the tallest boys in the village. This man towered so high that Jad knew that he could not really be a man. In his hand the man carried a long, golden crook that shone like the sun itself were inside.

Zua.

With his lush golden beard and his tall, tanned legs showing beneath his clean tunic—the hue of the sky on a sunny day—he looked exactly as Jad had always pictured him.

Fear rumbled up through Jad from miles beneath him. He dropped his chin back down to the grass. "Forgive me, Zua, for not believing as my father does," he said.

He waited with his head low. The rebuke would come.

Why else would the god Zua appear before me if not to punish me for being a wayward part of his flock? I'm no better than Miu, always running away.

Zua sometimes rewarded old shepherds who had kept their flocks safe, brought them peace and ease in ending, and punished those poor shepherds who strayed, leaving their flocks in harm. Those bad shepherds, he stranded them with their souls locked inside their bodies for the beasts of Zua's eternal forest to feed upon.

Would Zua use his golden crook to guide him gently nearer, or with the butt end push him away, as befit one who didn't deserve to be in Zua's flock?

I left my flock, Jad thought. *Alone with the lion near.*

And worse: his father had always warned him: *Stop asking so many questions. The sheep don't question the shepherd. You'll stray too far someday, boy, too far for Zua to bring you back.*

Jad's knees trembled. He should have listened to his father. He had been right.

Please, Zua, forgive your lost lamb, he prayed, as his father often called him.

As he knelt quaking in the grass, his knees wobbled; he really needed to pee. Large, sandaled feet thudded a couple of paces from his head. Zua was standing over him. Jad waited for the touch of the crook.

Push or pull?

When Zua passed him by, he raised his head and peered back beneath his arm. *Has he pushed me away?* Zua had stopped five paces behind him, bending low to Miu. She was here in Zua's pasture with him, chomping vigorously on the soft grass of perfect green like she'd never eaten before in her life.

Zua petted her woolly head, standing by her looking off into the distance, leaning on his golden crook. When the ewe moved a few paces away to keep grazing, the god did not move.

"Please … forgive your lost lamb," Jad said, aloud this time, hoping, but also fearing, to gain Zua's attention.

He waited, his blood beating like a drum in his ears in the breathless land.

"Zua … I'm here … Jad…" he said. And lowered his head, if not his eyes.

Zua's golden crook gleamed in the sun. *But where is the sun in this strange place?* Jad couldn't see it. There was only grass to the horizon, no trees, no other people. Formless lumps in the distance might have been other sheep grazing. The clouds above hung like a puff of cold breath. Every blade of grass looked the same, like little spikes.

He heard his father's voice: *Don't question him, fool,* and he lowered his head again.

He stayed that way for a few moments. Then Jad pushed to his knees, raising his eyes to gaze upon Zua directly. In his mind he could hear his father yelling at him. *Trust in Zua, boy! Why do you always have to stray?*

Zua did not seem to notice. Jad looked back toward the unmoving, treeless horizon. The air here smelled sweetly of fresh grass. It was peaceful. Yet … *this is wrong.*

He couldn't say how. But he knew.

Don't question the will of Zua, he could hear his father scolding. *Kneel, boy!*

No air pushed against him, and though he could see far into the distance, he felt closed in, as if he could reach out and touch two walls to either side of him.

Zua had saved Miu from her fall, but what did Zua do in this place?

Hearing movement behind him, Jad turned to see Zua bent over the patch of grass Miu had eaten. Where he touched, more grass pushed up from the ground, as perfect as the rest, creaking like leather as it rose. When it was the same height as all the rest, Zua stood rigidly again, a contented smile on his broad, bearded face, gazing off into the distance.

Trust in Zua, boy!

Zua looked like an idiot.

"Zua?" said Jad, waving, feeling invisible.

Jad stood, and Zua didn't budge. After a moment, Jad circled around him toward Miu.

It was like Zua didn't know he was there.

Remembering the lion then made his feet move. It didn't matter that Zua wouldn't talk to him, he had come to gather Miu. He had to get back. He had a flock to protect.

It was when Jad clutched Miu by the wool on the back of her neck to lead her that she bleated in surprise and Jad saw Zua's head turn his way.

A drop of fear made a long fall inside Jad. *Zua turned Miu's way—at the sheep,* Jad realized.

Then Jad saw Zua's eyes for the first time and he wished he really were invisible. Zua's cloudy, anvil irises, the same as the flock he watched over, turned their height upon him.

Stupid sheep, stupid sheep, stupid sheep, he remembered thinking.

A dumb haze of malice crossed Zua's wide, kindly face, the determined look Sham got right before she backed up and rammed his legs.

Get me out of here.

Zua's fingers, like cords of rope at the end of his long, muscular arms, tightened around the shaft of his long crook as the large man, his father's god, turned and took a step in his direction that quaked the land—*Zua's land*—beneath him. The sky dimmed. Somehow he knew that his desire to leave, his defiance, was souring the air of this place. It wasn't Zua's doing, and Zua didn't like that either. Those dumb anvil eyes burned into him.

Get me out of here. From somewhere came to Jad an understanding. *Yes,* he could do that. He could leave.

Jad saw the air quaver, shimmer, and Zua, too, wavering like a ripple in dark water. Zua came stomping big steps toward him, reaching for his neck with fingernails that each ended in nails that looked like little hooves.

Jad lost a step, hearing the echo of what sounded like a word spoken in the sky and in the rocks—*My voice?* It resonated from the flat, golden light, and from the blackness he saw when he closed his eyes.

Yes.

Then, just like the ravine before, Zua and everything around him ripped away—the unmoving, too-large sky, and the grass that stretched on forever. *Sheep paradise.* The ravine's bullying wind hit Jad like a shove in the back, ruffling his hair.

He was back. He huffed down big breaths, relieved. The ravine had returned, the drop just five paces from where he was wobbling. Its white water gnashed far below. Alive.

He felt a burning against his neck, and realized it was the lingering heat from Zua's fingers grasping for his throat.

Jad plunked down on a rock, the blood thumping in his ears nearly as loud as the rapids. There was a lot here he had never really noticed before: the wintery smell of the forever snow above, the dry musk of the dust swept high from the plains miles below, the nervous scent of the storm gathering over the far mountains. Added together, they smelled like home.

Miu put her head down, took a mouthful of grass, then spit it out and bleated.

Jad laughed. Too loudly. And then laughed at how it was too loud. After she had eaten the grass in sheep paradise, the thin blades by the ravine must taste like ... well, he didn't have a comparison for that. Not as good anyway. It would be a while before Miu came to appreciate ungodly grass again.

He led Miu from the ravine by the scruff of her neck. The fear had returned: the lion—*against which Zua won't be a help*—where was the lion? Zua didn't care about lions.

Or Jad's father who loved Zua so much, he realized. He didn't think Zua cared about anything but sheep and grass.

Zua is an idiot.

He hefted Miu, carrying her across his shoulders, moving much faster that way, starting with long loping strides back across the hillside of small, scrubby trees. By now he might have lost half the flock to the lion. The dread of that idea roiled in his belly.

Or the whole flock, if they couldn't flee farther than ten paces from the crook.

He might return to a massacre. *Would the guts and bones stay inside the circle as well?* He'd never be able to explain that to Father. And Father would know if he told a lie.

The same way he would know he was telling the truth about Zua.

He couldn't wait to tell Father about Zua.

Jad hauled Miu back to halt her from running to the flock. Milling inside the crook's circle, they were as annoyed and bored as he'd left him. Except a figure now stood atop the same rock he'd had his nap on.

His first thought jumped to, *Zua.* Obviously no. It was a short, skinny person.

Crouching among the wide gray slabs that littered the edge of the meadow, Jad inched closer until he reached a small, scruffy tree about a stone's throw distance, bobbing his head around like a little bird's to get a better look. The figure had found the crook jammed in the rocks and was spinning it in his hands. Then the figure turned and he saw it wasn't his father's crook he was holding. It was a spear. Someone that short with a spear, it could only be one person—Tez.

Jad let Miu go and she took off running directly toward the circling flock. *Will she have to stay inside the circle with the rest of them?* He doubted it.

Standing tall, he threw his shoulders back, unable to keep the smirk from his face. He had seen Zua. *Zua is an idiot,* he would tell Tez. All the way back, he had been practicing how he would say it. It was a way better story than the time Tez went with his father and the men to hunt down the Kratens who had stolen blankets and half a leg of mutton from the village—old Mrs.

Alm, they had beaten her black and blue while she was gathering berries. She had walked with a limp since that day, and her mouth drooped like old leather when she smiled.

You would have thrown up, Tez said every time he talked about it. *Like this.* And he'd retch and jab his tongue out. He always demonstrated the things Jad would have done. *And you would have cried when my father pulled back the Kraten woman's head and cut her throat. She kept crying like, "No, oh no, don't do it." And your da, he tried to stop him too, him and a few other of the woman-men from the village. But my da didn't listen to them. You should have seen him. He just hauled her hair back and* blurb-blurb-blurb, *all the blood came spilling out of her neck. There was so much of it. You would have been sick.*

Tez made a high-pitched voice for the woman, and never forgot to gurgle the blood sounds after he ran his finger across his neck, wiggling his fingers by his throat to be the blood spurting. The blood sounds weren't good. Cutting a person's throat, that was probably not much different than a sheep's. And he and Father had done that dozens of times. He wouldn't have been sick. Tez would be sick if he had to help birth a lamb and it came out back hooves first—sometimes buckets of blood came then, and he'd have to reach his arm inside, untangle the ewe's insides from around the lamb.

But when Jad said that the last time Tez had told his story about the Kratens, Tez just laughed and said, *You would have thrown up.*

Seeing Zua would be better than two stupid thief Kratens any day.

I saw Zua. And he was an idiot. He made a face like this. And he'd screw his face up, cross his eyes.

Jad got way closer to the flock than he thought he would before Tez gave a jolt of broken daydreams and stopped spinning his spear.

"Is that the one you like the most?" Tez called out, pointing at Miu. "Is that your special one, the one you kiss?" Still up on the rock, Tez started thrusting with his hips and bleating, "*Baar, baaar, barrrrr.*"

Jad tried calling out to him, to ask him why he was there, but Tez kept thrusting, "*Barrr, barr, barrr,* oh sheepy, sheep," louder and louder so that Jad couldn't say anything, until Jad made it all the way to the stone Tez was standing on.

Then Tez said, "Get your stuff. We got to go. There's a Phentinite army coming. Going to attack the village."

Tez walked in front of the flock, jabbing at bushes and stabbing the willowy tops from flowers, never letting the butt of his spear touch the ground. *It's not a walking stick*, Tez always said. Jad trotted back and forth, urging the sheep leaping and bleating onward.

Tez would never be as tall or as strong as his father, Jad had heard Mother saying to Father once. He had too much of his mother in him. *And talks ten times as much as she did*, Father had said, and Mother had laughed. *If only...*

Tez pushed his plump chest out, head high, as they descended the uneven trail, which with his short legs gave him a shambling, swaying walk—*Like a duck*, Jad secretly thought. Every so often Tez would stumble over a stone.

Jad called out to him: "How can you be scouting for the lion if you're only scouting straight ahead? If the lion is stalking us, it'll sneak up on us from behind. Haven't you ever seen a cat?"

Tez pretended not to hear, jabbing at a passing bee. He had barely seemed to care when Jad had told him about his night spent watching for the creature in the shadows.

Perhaps he'll start watching after Sham gives him a good punt from behind, Jad thought, watching the sheep cantering sidelong behind his friend, as if trying to line him up.

The tree's shadows had lengthened from daggers to spears by the time they drove the flock down near one of the lower plateaus and stopped at the river crossing—the same flat, peaceful water that farther up the mountainside roared through steep gorges, the same river by which Jad had met Zua.

The sheep fanned out to drink. They knew the crossing well. Jad hopped stone to stone across the river, low in late summer, remembering to not enjoy it as he wasn't a kid anymore.

Chasing strays the whole descent down the mountain, Jad hadn't thought about Zua, but as the sinking sun puckered down onto the western hills, he remembered Zua's crook burning with its inner golden light. If he had one like it, maybe they could make it home early, easily. The coming night would have stars and most of the moon—otherwise they'd never make it—but last night had been hard. He had been afraid. Tonight they would have to burrow slowly through that same darkness, and the back of his neck had been tingling all evening.

He looked up at his crook, imagining it glowing with a golden light, and clutched it tightly.

Tez had planted his spear—*but not like a walking stick*—making an impatient face at him. "Are you scared?"

"No," said Jad, startled out of his daydream. "Of what?"

"The Phentinites."

"Oh. No," said Jad offhandedly. They hardly seemed real.

Why would they come all this way? Jad's father had asked a trader just a few months ago. The Phentinite city was in a distant land that they only heard about from traders in Ren.

Jad's grandfather had come from the market town with the first founders of their village to settle up here in the hills, escaping the people who didn't approve of their worship of the great god Zua. A lot of people in Ren still gave him and Father wary looks when they came to town to sell their wool and their cheese. But the traders never cared, and spoke to them straight. None of them were ever from Ren anyway, usually from one of the cities farther down the shore of the great lake, doing business by boat rather than marching off inland to other towns and people with one of the long, dusty caravans.

They live in a city of thousands of people, the trader told them. *They worship Shangar, the god eater. I hear he sits on his enormous throne above the city. It's said their armies shake the ground as they march, their soldiers layered in gold and jewels. They're not so far away. They have a garrison in Copra, practically the next stop along the road.*

People like that, Father had asked, shaking his head, *what would they want here?*

Everything, said the trader with a smile, the bright beads in his beard jingling. *First, they ask for it with words. And if they don't get what they want with words, then they ask with spears.*

Truth or not, Father had hung on his every word, trying to show his blank bargaining face. These traders were known to say anything to make a deal.

The trader had pulled a white cloth from off a basket. *And because they asked the Spergians with spears last year*, the trader added, *I can give you a good deal on these dates.*

Father bought the dates. It was only fair for what was probably good information.

The horse lords will keep them away, Father said as they were concluding the deal. *If the Phentinites bring their armies onto the plains past the great lake, their war wagons will run them down. The Phentinites know better than that.*

The trader had shrugged his wide, padded shoulders. He had his own practiced, secret face.

"My father will take care of it," said Jad. "I'll see what he says."

"Your father couldn't take care of a fart," laughed Tez. "What's he going to—hey, who's that?"

Tez pushed past Jad, hopping upstream rock to rock, and when he turned, Jad just caught sight of a mat of black hair slipping behind a large, green-speckled rock in the middle of the river.

"Tez, stop!" he said, a cold shiver slicing through him head to toe. What if they were Phentinites? If Tez died right now, he still had to take care of the flock all by himself, and the sheep were milling on both sides of the crossing. "Tez!"

Tez is an idiot.

He ran after his friend, splashing through the shallow water, his eyes burning with greasy sweat, tipsy from the walking he had already done.

Tez had already reached the rock where they'd seen the person hiding. No axe had cleaved his brains all over the rocks yet. "Who are you?" Tez yelled, bringing his spear arm back. "What do you want here?" Jad saw a man's hands rise to protect himself.

The icy water gripped Jad's feet as he ran. *Tez is going to spear him.* He could hear it in his friend's voice. He was really going to do it.

Whoever hid behind the rock gabbled loudly back at Tez.

With a last lunge, Jad grabbed the butt of the spear just before Tez could get his weight behind it, halting it awkwardly by his ear.

Tez whipped around to him in a snarl, wrenching the spear out of his grasp. "What are you doing, idiot?"

Half propped up behind the green-speckled boulder, a man lay slumped in the stream, his hands a flurry to ward off Tez's blow. He warbled off a nervous tirade of words that Jad didn't understand. But it was no problem to tell he knew Tez had just tried to kill him.

"He could be a Phentinite spy!"

At that, the man's expression changed and his rambling stopped. He'd understood that word, *Phentinite*, and clearly was trying to convey he wasn't. He pointed to the hateful sneer on his face. It looked like he was trying to say he hated Phentinites.

The quick-running water pushed against the rock the man had chosen to hide behind, damming a small pool. Little worms of blood were curling into that calmness, tingeing the water pink. A strip on the man's thigh, cloth tied above it to staunch the bleeding, had split like raw steak. Above, a big daisy of blood splotched what used to be a white tunic, red trickling down the leather armor he wore over it, which was unlike any Jad had seen before. It was well made, even if darkened by the water and hanging from his thin frame like a harness.

"Look at him," said Jad. "He's injured. He's been in a fight."

"So?"

Jad had to admit Tez had a point. Few people ventured into this part of the mountainside except Zuans from his village, maybe men out herding or hunting, and the women picking berries. Above, the peaks were snowy, impassable, home to storms, practically unexplored, as there was nowhere on the other side of them that anybody wanted to reach. Just goats and eagles, furry lizards…

…*lions*…

Jad pushed himself between Tez and the man. Tez let him, but his spear never lowered, and Jad looked down at the shiny, sharp black point inches from his chest. More it was Tez now and not fear of the man behind him that shoved a shiver through him, even aware that if the man were to lean forward and lunge for him with a knife, the first he'd know of it would be when he saw the tip stab out through his chest.

His back tingled until Tez's spear half lowered, then he spun to face the man in the water. "Who are you?" he asked, firmly if not as harshly as Tez.

The man gaped up at him, eyes wide like those of a sheep wedged between two stones. He had a week's worth of beard, scraggly dark hair hanging down into his face. He didn't look like a spy, but if he were some kind of lost imbecile from Ren, or a trader's runaway slave, Tez was going to end up spearing him through the eye if he didn't say something useful soon.

"Jad," he told him, speaking slowly, pointing to himself. Establishing names was the first thing his father did when speaking to a new trader. It helped put them both at ease. "Tezza," he added, throwing a thumb over his shoulder at Tez, who didn't so much as grunt.

Removing his hand from his injured shoulder, the man patted his chest briefly, and again rattled off a long string of nonsense that Jad didn't understand.

"Look at his hands," said Tez, pointing. "He's a Rada. See his knuckles—they're metal." Now that he looked closer at the man's hand pressed to his bloody chest, Jad could see the man had what looked like dark metal fastened to the backs of all his knuckles, not *worn* he saw, but as if melded to his skin. "All Rada warriors have metal melted onto their hands when they're twelve or thirteen. It makes a weapon of his bare fist."

Tez sounded a little jealous, maybe awed. For good reason. Pouring metal on like that must have been excruciating. Not an imbecile or slave, then. A soldier.

"Rada is part of the Phentinite Empire," Tez growled. "I was right. We should kill him now, before he can find his way back and tell the army we're here."

Jad looked at the small pool growing ever pinker beneath the man. If the soldier was losing that much blood, he wouldn't live long enough to tell anybody anything. Besides, those wounds weren't from a bear, or a fall. That wound in the shoulder looked like a spear strike. What that meant, he wasn't sure. But either way, in his condition, if they left him here he'd probably last another day, two if he got dry.

The man was looking from Tez to Jad and back again. He coughed and protested, speaking quickly, though weakly, his hands in the air pointing at them and then to himself, waving, clasping.

Jad didn't need to understand the words to know he was pleading for his life. He closed his eyes and put his head down, thinking. Tez knew more about these things than he did. He was like a soldier too, in a way.

What would Father do if he were here?

Well, that much was obvious. He'd make an offering to Zua and then do what he thought was best.

He'd been trying not to get his feet wet. Now he watched a small fish circle his feet, the river's chill working up through his legs. He willed himself not to shiver. They had to get home as soon as possible, first to get the flock someplace safe, and now to tell them about this man.

It hit him then: *The Phentinites really are coming.*

Jad steeled himself, trying to keep the decision he had just made from his face, and knowing he was failing at it. He had to be strong if he was going to watch Tez drive a spear through this man's eye.

The Rada saw him thinking; his hands waved more animatedly. But Jad didn't hear him anymore.

If only we could talk to him...

Much like he had when he had sensed Zua's presence in the ravine, Jad thought he heard what was almost a word, assent rustling through the trees and riding on the wind, a trickle beneath the babble of the river, as if it were one voice in chorus with itself in different pitches.

"You're good boys," the man said then. "I can tell you're good boys. Raised right. Strong and healthy. You wouldn't hurt me, would you? I'm at your mercy."

Jad looked at Tez, whose face became three perfect circles, obviously as surprised as he was. Tez didn't deal with surprises well. Most emotions turned to anger.

"Why didn't you speak normal before?" Tez yelled. "Why all the sheep talk?"

The man sank lower into the water, losing grip on his wound as Tez surged forward. Blood oozed into the pool from his red hand.

"You speak Rada?" he said, amazed.

"No, we don't speak Rada! You speak like us," said Jad,

before Tez could punctuate his surprise with the tip of his spear.

Bewildered, the man looked to them both, holding up his metal-glazed knuckles of one hand. "I am a soldier of Rada. You boys, you must be from the village? There's only one so far up here into the hills. I escaped from the Phentinite army. They're coming to take your village. I can help, if you help me. Don't let me die here in this river. I can help."

Despite the Rada soldier being skinny and bedraggled, Jad stumbled through the dark, arm in arm down the rocky and overgrown path with him. Tez, not stabbing dandelions anymore, trailed five paces behind them, spear held at the ready.

You want to bring him back, I'm not carrying him. You have to do it. I'll be here to spear him when he takes his chance to stab you in the neck.

It occurred to Jad that if just yesterday they had come across a man bleeding in the river, they would have helped him. Almost without thinking. Dragged him out of the river. Tried to dress his wounds. Tez probably would have run back home to fetch a few more men who might have even built a litter. With help, it would be easy to guide the flock home then.

Now he was wondering if he was wrong to be helping. Tez wasn't watching the sheep and they were scattering all over the place.

When he visited Ren, Jad liked to watch the blacksmith huffing the forge's bellows, heat belching from the fire and scorching the ground. Now, as he stumbled along with the man's weight, it felt like he'd taken a couple of those hot orange rods out of the coals and shoved them up into his legs to use as bones.

A few times he had thought about suggesting Tez go for help. He would bargain with himself: *He wouldn't be gone long. I could wait here with the guy. Tez would be back by dawn. I could gather the flock back together...*

Then he would picture the soldier drawing a knife and punching it up into his neck. Or smashing his teeth in with a rock like cracking ice. The man was thin, weak from loss of blood, but still a man, and he was just a boy. *And maybe he's faking?*

We should have searched him.

He focused on being tall, strong. The man had hardly said a thing since they'd began walking. Times they stumbled, Jad saw his teeth clench, pain flash across his face.

Was it too late to stop and search him now?

Since yesterday, it was like an invisible veil had dropped from the sky. The light had paled, smells muted. The world looked thinner, and Jad's eyes flitted object to object in the dimness. These inlets and glades along the path, once familiar as family, were strangers to him now. He missed yesterday, before Zua, before the Phentinites, the man, the lion, when the only thing he had to worry about was a wayward ewe or dew-dampened bread. The sharp itch he'd felt while searching for Miu, like they were being watched, had worsened too. Even with the strain and discomfort of holding up the heavy soldier, when they stopped it nagged at him.

Passing through a flat clearing in the woods, one that Jad knew was near the base of the mountainside, the man fell against him, drawing him down.

"Rest, boy. I need to rest. My leg is like a block of wood."

Jad didn't want to argue. He had nearly torn his shoulder off when they'd stumbled, and he needed to gather the sheep.

"Get up and keep moving," Tez barked behind them, the same sharp voice he'd been using for the past few hours—a poor imitation of his father. Jad leaned against a tree. Tez was a blob in the darkness, but the smooth stone tip of his spear caught the moonlight.

"I need to loosen this binding," said the soldier. "I'm not getting any blood into my leg. It'll stale and fall off."

"I don't care about your leg," growled Tez. "Get him up," he ordered Jad.

"You want my help, boy." It was not a question. The soldier dragged himself up onto a fallen log, already reaching to untie the strip of leather keeping his leg from bleeding. "You're a strong boy, that's plain to see. One of the strongest boys I've ever seen. You'd make a fine warrior of Rada. But the Phentinites, even my people couldn't stand up to their armies. We needed help and we didn't have any. I'm here to help you."

In the stillness, they heard the soldier's leather binding strap flap onto the log. Black shone darkly on the grass. The soldier groaned, rigid, kicking his other foot against a stone.

"You want to keep your legs, right, boys? Well, I want to keep my leg too. Just a minute's rest. Good boys like you would let me rest just a minute. You're strong and don't need to rest, but I'd let you rest if you got a chop to the leg by a stinking traitor."

Traitor?

Jad stretched his shoulders to ease the tingling there, which had grown strong again. Maybe he was just nervous, tired, hungry. Things were different. He needed a moment's rest, then he'd go back to fetch the sheep. By now, half the flock was probably fumbling through the darkness. It wasn't quite a meadow they had just passed through, but a place where the trees were older and the brush on the ground sparse and low. Not a perfect grazing spot, but there were worse places to gather them back together.

"I'll just be a minute, boys. Then you can show me your fine home." The soldier sucked in a harsh breath as he flicked old blood from the leather binding, cinching it tight around his leg again. "If the great god Ardo doesn't call me home first."

Tez had been unusually quiet lurking there in the darkness. It seemed he too had been thinking. "Tell me about the Phentinites," Tez said.

The soldier leaned back, bending his leg with another groan, stretching it out. "I know everything there is to know about them," he said. "What do you want to know?"

"They have a great empire," said Tez. "And they're coming to attack us."

The soldier raised a finger. He had a crooked smile. "That is true. You're a smart boy. If there's any one thing that could be said about the Phentinites, it's exactly that." Jad could see the soldier looking from him to Tez. "Of course, you know about their city of Eriim. It sits in the embrace of the mountain of Shangar, the god eater. Some say the god eater is only a story, but it's true, boys. I've seen the city. I have seen Shangar. I thought it was just a tale to scare children, but when the Phentinites came and took me from my home ... imagine walls taller than these trees, and five paces thick. Atop them are towers carved with the likenesses of all the gods of other peoples they've captured. They had us marching in a row, like we were chained together. They marched us up to their gigantic gates. There they stopped us, and we looked up, and we saw them perching the face of our great god Ardo up above their western walls. They wanted us to see."

"You let them take your god?"

"They take gods, boys—not yours, I'm sure, but many—into the embrace of Shangar. That's what they call stealing the gods of the people they conquer: taking them into the *embrace* of Shangar. Eriim, it is as huge a city as any I've ever seen. It has as many people as there are grains of sand on the beach ... or grass in a meadow..." The soldier groaned as he shifted his legs. "The entire great mountain behind the city of the Phentinites ... Shangar sits there ... carved from the very stone, the peaks of his crown touch the clouds. If Shangar were to let go of the great city and stand, he could grab the moon from the sky ... probably just to eat it..."

The soldier looked from Tez to Jad, maybe waiting for them to say something. Neither of them did. Probably like Jad, Tez was numbed by the enormity of what the soldier was saying.

"What do they want from us?" Jad heard himself asking. His people weren't important. Jad had always known that. They were only a small village.

He rubbed the back of his neck. The itch had returned so strongly that it felt like a burning ember had landed on him.

Some of the flock had ambled down the path ahead. They knew the way home; they stopped here often. More were losing and finding one another in the thin copse of trees behind them, *baaing* to one another in the pale, peaceful starlight.

If weak, the soldier still had keen, piercing eyes. Jad didn't like how they roved over him.

"What does a flood want with a puddle, or a stream? The Phentinites are like their hungry god. They spread over the land from their great city. If they do not have to conquer ... like the rising waters, they absorb you into them. You pay to become Phentinite. Just a little part, a small rivulet into the great whole."

"And what if you fight?" blurted Tez, too loudly for the hush of the late hour.

"Then they eat you. Their god feeds on your god."

Jad didn't know what to think of that, and looked to Tez. But Tez simply leaned on his spear and Jad couldn't read anything in his stillness.

The soldier sucked in a gasp of pain. "Tell me about your worthy village, boys. Do you have many men of fighting age? How many men with bows? Do you have skilled hunters? How about—?"

"We don't speak to spies," growled Tez. He paced back and forth in the crunchy leaves. "Or weaklings who let their god be taken to be ... to be *eaten*." He spat the word like it had clotted in his mouth.

Jad rubbed his hand over the back of his neck.

"Hey ... hey," said the soldier, "peace ... peace ... of course *your* worthy village will have many mighty warriors such as yourself. But tell me, I've heard it said that many speakers hail from these barbarian lands. Is that true? Are you lucky enough to have a speaker? An army might divert like a stream around a mighty boulder if they know there's a speaker. They would be afraid their little worms would rot off, or the eyes would melt, or they'd shit out th—"

Tez sprang forward, spear brandished at the Rada's face. "We're not like your heathen people, Rada," he growled. "We're not blasphemers or magic fools, heretics against the protection of Zua. Zua is strong! Your invaders will break against Zua!"

Rearing back from Tez, the soldier fell onto the crunchy branches and leaves and whimpered, not just in pain. "I can help you, I can help," he said in a small voice, his hand held up not quite touching the tip of Tez's spear.

Tez had pushed after him, his chest heaving. "With Zua's blessing, we will stab every last one of their soldiers in their heathen faces!" His spear wavered guts to neck to eyeballs and the Rada's hand followed.

I should stop him, Jad thought. He had never heard Tez speak much about Zua, but this time his scowl didn't seem to be for show.

He closed his eyes. The burning in the back of his neck...

Is my head falling off?

He had to walk. He padded past Tez in the dim light—who by his sidelong look he thought might be waiting for him to stop him from spearing the soldier. He leaned by the gate of trees they had come through back along the path, looking for the ghostly figures of the flock's stragglers grazing between the tall, pale, scaly trunks of the trees. He listened. Something felt wrong. The burning sank from his neck and into his body, deeper, spreading out, less a burn and more an ache.

He hated it. *What is it?*

And when the answer came to him, it felt obvious.

Oh no. He should have paid attention. He should have *listened.*

His crook was in his hands. Without thinking, he hefted it high, jamming it down hard into the soft leaf litter. "Come to me!" he yelled to the sheep lingering in the woods, not knowing how he knew but understanding that they would hear him and come to the crook.

Too late, you idiot.

His yell broke the night. Bushes crackled, leaves scattered. The lion burst from the gray haze between the big trees as if a huge hungry claw had risen from the forest to smash against the grazing flock. The panicked sheep shook through the undergrowth, bleating terror and rattling the smaller trees. Jad counted six or seven stragglers trampling toward him. But not fast enough.

The lion had been waiting in the tallest of the bushes, and when enough of the flock drew close, it had pounced, easily catching the nearest ewe almost before it could turn and run.

Jad had heard animals dying before, dozens of times. All creatures, when dying, screamed, whether it be a sheep or a bird or a person. They resisted. They know it's death come for them and screech against it. For help? He was never sure. It didn't matter. He hated it. It was the worst sound in the world. And now he heard it again, the sheep's screams cleaving down through him, embedding in his soul, mercifully cutting off as the lion lunged high and bore down hard, snapping the sheep's neck.

It's my job to help them, he thought. *I protect them.*

He didn't move. There was nothing he could do against this.

Nor was the lion done. It rose like fog from the black soup of what used to be one of his flock and lunged between the trees, long muscular lopes leaping after another small white smear that was running toward its shepherd—*Miu*, Jad realized. He didn't know how he could tell in the darkness, but that little sheep was Miu. Running toward him for safety.

Run, Miu!

It was his job to protect his flock.

Too late.

Miu didn't have time to scream. The lion fell upon her like a foot upon rotten fruit. Lunged for her throat and bore down; its wide paws, toes spread, claws extending, covered half the little ewe's body.

Jad heard the crunch and saw the shining blood spurt onto the newly fallen leaves.

Called to the crook, the rest of the sheep had retreated behind him. The lion's hunched shoulders, nearly as tall as Jad, rose from its kill. Five paces long, the largest creature he had ever seen, a monster, its wide, maneless face had long, possibly old scars running from eye to muzzle where it had been raked with claws. Hunger reeked from it. It had stalked them all the way down out of the mountain's summer pastures—perhaps cast out from its pride, maybe even come down through one of the mountain passes—a creature from another place. The cage of ribs standing out against its long, lean, body were a remnant of its journey. The lion stood there looking at Jad as if it had farther it wanted to go.

This is what Zua is supposed to protect us from, Jad realized.

The lion's piercing, patient eyes fell on him, roving from belly to neck, and Jad was aware of the night's darkness around him more than he ever had been, and where Tez and the soldier stood somewhere behind him—his fellow flock.

This is how the sheep feel, looking to the herd for help. To the shepherd. To him.

But these sheep had a sleeping shepherd. *Zua is an idiot.*

His grip tightened on his crook. He met the huge lion's unwavering gaze. "Go," he told it flatly. The black pits of its eyes stayed on him. "Go," he told it again, pointing into the darkness. "You got what you wanted."

The lion's wide tongue licked the blood from its muzzle. Its huge paws lifted a few steps. It turned, cast one last sidelong look at him, clamped Miu's body in its broad mouth, and trotted away with her, as silent as steam. In the dim light, Jad couldn't follow. One moment it was lurching through the trees, the next it had become the night again.

He turned around. "We need to go," he whispered to Tez and the soldier.

All the flock, having been called to the crook, even if they had been safe and happy farther down the path to home, had come back, and were facing him, *shepherd, protector*, their dumb faces all in a line, silent, eerie, judging. Jad could taste the awful acrid tang of blood that hung in the air.

The soldier remained sprawled over the log where he had fallen. He couldn't get up without help. Tez had retreated five paces behind him, his spear braced low in two hands. Seeing him, he heard Tez's father berating him: *Hold high to strike. Holding low is only good for your own little pokers.* At first rigid as rock, Tez's expression mirrored the sheep to either side of him, staring on mutely, then his shoulders melted, the tip of his spear wavered. Slowly he raised it to the appropriate high hold of readiness, before the tip sank all the way to the scratchy leaf litter at his feet. His face, still smeared with shock, slackened, drawing up into clenched teeth.

The sheep stayed silent, looking back past Jad with their knowing, anvil eyes.

"It'll come back for the other sheep it killed," said Jad evenly. "After that, if we're still here, it'll take all of us."

The rest of that night they stumbled through an ageless dark, Jad supporting the bleeding soldier, Tez somewhere behind them with a prodding spear, the flock milling before them like ghosts flitting across the path and floating through the trees.

Jad kept coming back to the same thought: *Maybe we're in Zua's eternal forest now. Zua saw that I strayed. Now all of us will be punished. The beasts of the forest will feast on our bodies. The lion is still out there, behind us. And now he'll come for us too.*

He didn't really believe that. Still, as the night went on and his limbs sagged and his eyes dragged in the dirt, he listened for the click of claws on rock, a low growl. Dawn came with the relief that the ghosts in the trees became sheep with morning; he could see more than just the soldier's white teeth and eyeballs near his shoulder. Red rose to coat the bottom of the sky, and eventually, when the sun poked above the horizon, golden light fell across them, dissolving the last of the night's shadows, and the dread that swirled in Jad's belly with them.

A lion. A terrible lion. That's all it was. Zua is an idiot, he muttered under his breath.

But even the calm the morning brought couldn't make the soldier any lighter, or the man's stench less terrible, like raw meat and old blood. Tez still wouldn't help, and Jad started counting his steps to distract from the pain in his legs, his numb shoulders. Each step came as a surprise. Eventually, he couldn't count any higher.

One ... two. One ... two.

Then he heard a voice say, "Tez, Jad—who is that?"

Jad lowered to his knees. *Far enough.*

He could hear fast water fluting into a rock someplace. Jad looked up and around. They had entered the clearing their grandparents had used for its tall, straight trees to build Zua's house when founding their village all those years ago. Tall bushes had since grown up, and from behind one of them Masom, Methen's son, stepped out onto the path ahead, from where he had apparently been watching. Masom, like Tez, instead of a crook was carrying a spear. Strange to see soft-spoken Masom with a weapon in his hand. It looked like he had rubbed his face with black dirt, which sweat had since streaked down his forehead and cheeks. Jad had always liked Masom well enough, even if he didn't always like to be around him overlong. Older than he and Tez by a few years, and tall and strong like his father, Masom tended to be straightforward in his thinking, and the games he played were more often rough, win or lose by who was last, who suffered first.

Dropped in the middle of the rocky path, the soldier didn't protest. He peered up at Masom warily. In the fresh light, his face looked as pale as a trout's belly.

"He's a Phentinite spy," said Tez, before Jad could catch his breath.

"No ... Phentinite," groaned the soldier on the ground through clenched teeth, trying to sit up.

"I didn't hear what he said," said Masom, looking from Jad to Tez. "Except Phentinite."

"He said he's a Phentinite spy," said Tez.

"Shut up, Tez," said Jad.

Stronger this time: "No ... *Phentinite*," the soldier repeated, pivoting to look up at Masom.

Next to him, arms wobbly, Jad shifted, keeping his distance

as Masom pointed down at the soldier. To his credit, he didn't point with his spear. "Who is he, Jad?"

"Rada," said Jad. It was taking forever to catch his breath. "Says he came here with the Phent'nites—escaped them." His tongue felt like one of the rain-revealed cobblestones he was sitting on. "That's how he got hurt. Fighting them. We found him in the river."

The soldier was looking at Jad as well. "Rada," said the soldier, holding up his metal fist.

"Says he knows where the Phentinites are. Wants to help."

"Well, I know where the Phentinites are," said Masom. "I got sent out to find them, and—"

"You found them?" blurted Tez. "Where are they?"

"Yeah," said Masom. "They're—"

Jad held up his hand. "Wait, Masom … ask him…" He pointed to the Rada.

It took a second for Masom to understand what he wanted. Tez, it seemed, didn't catch on. "Where are they, Masom?" he urged excitedly. "Tell me."

Masom stepped up near the soldier's outstretched feet. The soldier peeped up at him, just for a moment, loosening the strap around his leg, the pain drawing him down. In the flat, mist-tinted light, his leg looked black with thick new blood oozing slowly down over the ugly flaking smears of yesterday.

"You say you want to help, Rada? Where are the Phentinites?"

The soldier stared blankly up at Masom, shaking his head. He turned to Jad. "What did he say?"

"What do you mean? He asked you where the Phentinites are."

The soldier drew his hands down his face, rubbing his eyes. "Last I saw," he said, addressing Masom again, calmer than Jad thought he really was, "they were encamped near a lake, only a day out of Ren. We were following the river. We were told there'd be a large waterfall. There was a guide. From Ren. This was…" He sat back, counting on his fingers. "…twenty hours ago."

Jad looked up at Masom for verification. He hoped so, for the sake of his aching shoulder.

"That right, Masom?"

"I don't know," said Masom, screwing his face up as if Jad's question were stupid. "What did he say?"

"Don't be dumb, Masom," said Tez. Jad hadn't noticed when Tez had shifted over behind the soldier, spear raised at the back of the man's neck. "He right?"

"He didn't say anything. Just baby talk. You understood him?"

Tez's spear tip wavered. Jad had never seen Masom look so confused. He had long been studying to take over as Zua's man in their village from his father. Answers came easy for him.

The soldier was looking back and forth between Jad and Masom. "He doesn't talk like you boys," he said.

Jad shook his head. "He does."

"You understand him?" asked Masom. "This isn't time for tricks." He looked annoyed.

Jad stood, his legs weak, his head swimming. He thought it important to stand so Masom would believe him. "He said they left Ren two days ago. They had a guide, someone from Ren. They were going to follow the river to the waterfall."

Masom chewed on his lip. "Maybe," he said. "It doesn't matter. I have to get back and tell my dad and everyone. They're waiting on me. I suppose waiting on *us* now." He pointed at the soldier. "Let's get him up. He might be useful."

Jad vowed never to think ill of Masom again.

Masom could be rash, impulsive, blunt. Jad didn't like to be around him for too long. But when Masom hooked the gaunt soldier's other arm over his shoulder, Jad could walk without his bones crunching like dead leaves with every step. Today he loved tall, blunt Masom.

Soon the forest path widened. Around mid-morning, smoke came curling up from behind the trees. Hanging between them, the soldier lifted his head from where it had been bobbing like a branch in the wind, his face pinched in pain. Sheep kept stopping to lap his blood from the trail behind them.

As they came around the last bend in the path toward home, Jad found himself trying to see it through the soldier's eyes. The Rada came from a land so far away they barely had a name for it. He had passed through great cities, spoke with strange peoples. *Burning, plundered cities.* Before them now was their smattering of homes piled up from the surrounding stones and mud, supported with high timber roofs. A not-important place. Dust kicked up in the paths between buildings. More sheep and goats than people milled about in their dozen or so broad corrals on the other side of town—Jad could smell them already. To the Rada, the village must look pathetic, defenseless.

Why are the Phentinites even coming here?

But Jad could also see how the site for the town was chosen

well. High above the plains, they reaped the benefits from the timber that lined the great mountains, but they weren't so elevated that the snow crippled them for too many months of the year. There was plenty of pastureland here, ensuring their family homes were far apart, and more meadows above as the spring snows retreated. Years ago, after they moved here from Ren, their grandparents had coaxed the swift-running river into large pools where there were always plenty of fish, clams, and sometimes little crabs beneath the rocks. The wind over the river kept the worst of the summer's bugs away, and never was the village in the mountains' shadows so that night came looming over them in the middle of the afternoon.

In the center, Zua's house stood tallest, sided by Zua's altar of rams' skulls peering over their small village square, where his cousin Endo was kicking a ball around with Miu's friend, Suba. They soon saw them approaching the edge of town, called out, and the commotion that arose was like throwing a wad of fat into a hot pan. Heads sprouted from windows. A low rumble started. Where a moment before the village center had seemed empty, now four, five, six handfuls of people came rushing toward them.

The hot pokers rammed up into Jad's knees had long since cooled, rusted. He pulled up short, Masom and the soldier nearly toppling. "Jad?" someone called, a lone woman's voice. Angry voices were hailing Masom, both men and women, shouting. "Who is that, Masom? Phentinite! Masom captured a Phentinite!"

"A spy!" Tez yelled. "We caught him! We caught a Phentinite spy!"

Jad blinked hard. Now that he'd made it home he felt faint, the sky and the river shrinking with darkness. The Rada stumbled, and Jad nearly fell when the weight of the soldier lifted from him.

Bodies crowded around, shoving him.

"Phentinite!" someone hissed. A girl's voice near to him.

"Rada ... Rada," the soldier insisted in a raspy staccato like a cough. "Rada!" His loose armor made for easy handholds to be pulled and yanked. Jad found himself peering through arms and bodies, seeing the Rada's legs stretching out behind him as he was dragged. The man was clutching at the neck of his leather armor, which had hitched up around his throat.

"Rada! Rada!" he gasped, with pain like he was choking.

"A spy!" Tez was yelling behind Jad, his voice creaky, cranky, underused. "We caught him! Bash his head in!"

Jad heard a loud thump, like someone were beating a rug, and a groan from the soldier, his protests growing distant.

"Rada," said Masom, his calm demeanor like a rock in the river of the excited voices around them. "He's Rada. From their army. Injured. See his leg? Look at his knuckles."

Jad's sheep were excited, calling out to the others they were hearing in the corral on the other side of town.

"Jad? Jad?" said a warm, kindly voice next to him. A hand rubbed his arm. "He doesn't look good. Is he okay, Masom?"

"He's fine," said Masom over his shoulder, following the crowd that had taken the soldier from them.

"Just tired," said Jad, trying to follow Masom—they had struggled so long, the two of them, saving the soldier; he needed to see the job done, all the way home—but someone had a hold of his arm, and he turned to look up into the face of his mother's sister, Beatti.

Jad looked behind him. Tez was gone. They were alone now.

He couldn't let Tez stab the Rada in the face with his spear.

Not after we came all this way.

"Endo!" Aunt Beatti called out for his cousin.

Jad didn't want to see Endo, but in a moment Endo was standing there, small, skinny, peering Jad in the face like he was a bug under a rock he'd just turned over.

"Take Jad's sheep to their corral," said Aunt Beatti, pulling

Endo upright by the nape of his neck. Endo never said much around the adults. He turned to watch the crowd dragging the soldier toward Zua's shrine. "Do it!" said Aunt Beatti, pointing toward where a few of the sheep were milling in the trees. Endo took off at a run, kicking a rock skittering up the path.

Aunt Beatti led Jad down toward the village and sat him on the log where the older men, old Zuans like Marl, Methen's father, liked to scratch games in the dirt with long sticks. For the moment, they were nowhere in sight. Everyone was gathered by Zua's shrine, shouting.

"Stab him in the face!" he registered Tez yelling shrilly. "Kick him!"

Aunt Beatti was quick to come back with water, and passed him a small slab of cheese and some bread. He had been splitting his meager bit of dried meat with the Rada since the day before. Long hours he had been famished, then the hunger had faded and he'd felt like a tree that had rotted on the inside but stayed standing, rigid and hollow.

The cheese and water came like a sharp breath to a drowning man. He looked up at Zua's house, at the backs of everyone gathered, quiet now, who must be looking down at the soldier in their midst, by the altar.

"That better?" asked his aunt, and it was only then that Jad realized his mother was standing next to her as well, regarding him quietly.

Jad nodded. He finished the water in a single gulp, and his aunt went to fetch more.

"Is he really a spy, Jad?" his mother asked, arms folded.

Jad shook his head. "No. Maybe. Not a very good one."

His aunt came back with a full skin of water. The cheese creaked as he sank his teeth in. His mother and aunt were looking toward Zua's shrine. Tension in his chest glowed like hot embers, and Jad wiped red smears across his eyes.

He gave a little jerk. His father and Tez's father, and Methen,

Zua's keeper, were standing a few paces in front of him, next to his mother and aunt. Everybody had spread out to turn his way, the soldier too, on the ground, leaning up, the whites of his eyes clear even at thirty paces, in them now the same fear he'd seen last night in the river, hands fluttering to protect against Tez's spear.

"Is it true you boys brought him down?" asked Tate, Tez's father.

His father leaned in. His beard had grown shaggy in the handful of days that he was gone. "Are you okay, Jad?"

"Exhausted," said Aunt Beatti.

Tez's father shot her a harsh look. "The boy's old enough to answer for himself."

Kids were scared of Tez's father. He was wide, with broad shoulders and a thick neck, his hands the size of a child's face, but mostly it was his loud, brash, gruff voice, that scared children, like he only knew how to yell, and only knew how to ask questions even when there wasn't really a question he was asking.

Jad looked around him. His flock was gone. *Endo*, he remembered, had taken them. He had brought his flock home. But then he sank. *Not all of them.*

He nodded. It wasn't good to keep Tez's father waiting. "The lion got two of the sheep."

"Lion?" said his father.

"We don't care about the sheep, Jad," said Tez's father. "We—"

"The Phentinite," said Methen, ignoring how Tez's father scowled at him—it wasn't a good idea to interrupt Tez's father, Jad thought with a distant pang of amusement.

Methen was not as tall as his son, Masom, and thinner, and didn't have the same smirk—not in his face anyway, maybe in the way he held himself, the way he walked. "Masom said you boys found him. That true, Jad?"

Jad nodded again with a mouthful of cheese. He told them how they had seen the man in the river, already injured.

Before Jad could say much more, "This could be Zua's will that this man be here," said Methen, exchanging a look with Jad's father. "How else would we explain it? Go on, Jad."

"They're lying about something," said Tez's father.

Jad shook his head. He told him how the soldier said he was a Rada, not a Phentinite, and—

"How do you know?" growled Tez's father. "How do you know what he's saying? He's back there on the ground not even talking like a man, just *barr, barr, barr.*"

"We're not saying you're lying, Jad…" said his father.

Tez's father tromped in, grabbing him roughly by the arm. "Get up, boy," he grunted. "Come here." He pulled him over to where everyone was watching.

The Rada looked terrible. Wet and cold when they had found him, and chilled ever since, his skin looked as loose-fitting as his armor now. He had black bags under his eyes.

The Rada lifted one hand toward him. "Good boy," he said, "tell them I'm not a Phentinite. I want to help. They are coming."

The man reminded him of the half-drowned cat he and Tez had once found down in the river, looking up at them too tired to move, its eyes holding fear and resignation at their approach. *Stop poking it, Tez,* he had said when Tez kept nudging it with his spear. Jad had petted it. He could see the cat wanted to swat at his hand but it had given up. Tez's spear would poke in from beside Jad and jab the cat and it wouldn't move. He and Tez had gotten in a fight, rolling on the ground. Tez had stomped home, and when Jad had come back, the cat had gone.

Jad repeated what the man asked. Only then did the Rada relax, lowering his cheek down to the ground. Blood trickled from his nose down into the dust, where drops clotted into black balls.

"How do you know what he's saying?" boomed Tez's father, and there were murmurs from everyone looking on. The Rada peeped despondently at the corral of people around him. Jad had known everybody present all his life; they were his whole world, and he had never seen such anger shared over and between their faces, like the wriggling shadow in a hot bed of coals. They looked at Jad now in the same wary way the people of Ren did when he went with Father to do their trading. A few of them held spears, butts in the dust. Masom was the only other person standing within their circle, behind the soldier. He was holding the village's killing hammer, the one they used to brain a sheep before they sheared it, skinned it, and shared its meat.

Jad shrugged, looking at Tez, who had come up to stand in the shadow of his father. "He spoke funny to us at first too. But then he started speaking normal."

Tez's father looked down at Tez. His big hand, hard as a rock, fell on his son's shoulder, making him look up to meet his eye.

Jad's father stepped forward, next to Jad, bending down to look the Rada in the eye. "Where are they? Where are the Phentinites?"

The Rada looked at Jad, and Jad repeated the question, and then repeated what the Rada said—the same thing he had said on the trail when they had met Masom: a guide from Ren was showing them the way.

"Traitors to their own people. Only care about gold," growled Methen.

"They're not our people," said Jad's father, and there were murmurs of agreement.

Methen looked up at his son. "Masom?"

Masom nodded. "I waited along the river, atop the waterfall. They came up the valley and made camp, right about where he was saying. About a hundred men, with a few pack men. Didn't see a guide, but that didn't mean there wasn't one."

"When do you think they'll be here?" asked Jad's father.

"Waterfall is a day's walk. Tomorrow … tomorrow morning," said Masom.

"If they don't push on all night and try to kill us in our sleep," said Tez's father.

"Ask him," said Methen, and Jad realized he was talking to him. "Will they push on all night?"

The Rada had been looking man to man as they spoke. Now his wide, white eyes grabbed on to Jad as if he were on a tether and if he looked away he would fall.

"No, no, they will want to talk first," said the Rada eagerly. "Why fight when a town might give them all they want just because they come? That's why they bring a hundred men when thirty might do. Good boy, tell them I want to help. Tell them."

"Why should we trust him?" asked Tez's father.

"We should kill him," said one of the women behind him. *His mother's voice?* The Rada looked past him, up at her. He might not speak their words, but Jad thought he understood that. Tez had been saying it all the past day.

His voice like rocks grating together, the Rada told them how he had deserted from the Phentinite camp. Jad repeated as closely as he could.

"Everywhere they go," the Rada said, "they bring death, they bring corruption." The big man in his home city of Radene sold his honor for Phentinite gold. "We all gathered and they drew lotteries, and we were told one of our family had to go fight for them. I have a wife, my brother didn't. He was a good brother. He would hold his nose and never fight too hard for them…"

The Rada spit a sticky, bloody gob that he had to pinch from his lip with his fingers. He told them how a year later the big man in Radene came to their tannery. "Dirty work … honest business. He came and said my brother had been killed by the Phentinites. That lying pig told us he wasn't a good soldier.

That pig said many of the men from Radene were killed for laziness. My brother would never be killed for laziness. He was a strong warrior. Tell them, Jad, how he was a true warrior of Rada—the best of Rada—and they took him and used him like a rag to blow their noses, then they threw him away."

As weak as he was, the man could still clench his fists. His front teeth were rimmed with black blood.

"Do you see?" the soldier said, looking around the circle. "We are alike. The Phentinites came for me too. I had to go in my brother's place. I fought them. They dragged me out of my home. They knocked down my wife. Kicked her. My little girl—she is about this boy's age, the prettiest girl in all of Rada—she hid in the tree behind our house and I saw her watching. They took me and made me fight for them because they lied about my brother…"

To Jad it seemed silly simply repeating everything the man said exactly as he had spoken it. It felt like a trick; someone was laughing at him. But one look around at the scowls and scared children, how the Rada himself still dripped red into the dirt beneath him—*This is not a trick*. At least not on him. There might still be a trick on them all if he really was a spy, like Tez said, but Jad didn't believe that. The Rada would die here in the dirt, right in front of him.

Tired, Jad imagined he was speaking to his father, who always listened, so he wouldn't feel so shy when the Rada had more to say.

"The big man in Radene … me gone, my brother gone … I keep thinking of him coming to our house, waggling his fat, soft belly, offering to buy it—buy it with Phentinite gold—and when my wife, Tela, says no … Tela is there now all alone…" The Rada raised his fist for everyone to see. "Men like him, they won't stop until they own the whole world. They're like the Phentinites too. They stuff their fat faces full. They eat my dinner, then they eat your dinner. Most of the men coming here are Rada," said the soldier, turning to look up at Masom, who was still leaning on the long, heavy, hammer. "I tried to convince them this was wrong. 'We should be in our own country,' I told them. 'We don't belong here. We can fight the Phentinites and make the Rada people strong again.' What was happening to my family, it is happening to their homes too.

"Cowards … fools … they told me we couldn't take back our homeland … but I have to go back," said the Rada, eyes traveling face to face. "We shouldn't be in this land. I tried to run but they caught me, speared me. See, here—" He pushed against the web of a wound on his shoulder. "See this slash on my leg? But I got away," he said, "and if they leave here—or don't leave here—I can slip away, go home. I can help—tell them, boy."

How can he help? Jad heard someone whisper. *He's half chopped to pieces.*

Jad didn't think the Rada's story had the effect he wanted. Rada, fierce warriors from the west, if they were coming here as slaves to a greater empire, what chance did that leave them? They were herders, gatherers. Sheep they had hundreds, men they had no more than three handfuls.

"What are they saying, boy?"

"Stop calling me *boy*," said Jad. It was so unfair these warriors were coming to kill his people. *Why can't they just leave us alone?*

He didn't like how the Rada never met his eye. He and Father had come across a fox once, one that was acting oddly, rolling in the leaves, skittering sideways and falling over, but its snout ever pointing at them, teeth bared. Father told him not to go near it. *It's sick*, he said. *Don't let it bite you, or you'll end up crazy like that too*, his father said. The Rada gave him the same sense. He was skittering sideways, always keeping his snout turned towards him—except hiding his teeth.

A hand fell on his shoulder. Methen's. "Ask him again what

they want, Jad. Our grandparents came here to get away from Ren and be closer to Zua. That is our real treasure. What could they possibly want from us?"

Jad remembered what the soldier had said the night before about the Phentinites and their terrible god. He wanted to go home, so rather than say everything twice, "To eat us," he told Methen tiredly. "And eat Zua."

Everybody started talking around him before he had even finished. The Rada waved his arms at him, and for the first time tried to sit up, slipping, failing, collapsing into the dirt.

"No, no, not *eat* you, b—Jad. They want to make you part of their empire. If you pay them, you become Phentinite too. But they will take your god to be sure you pay, take your Zua." He gestured at Zua's shrine and fell back to the dirt.

Oh... Jad laughed, realizing his mistake. Not really *eat*. His laughter sounded odd amongst the worried gabble. He patted Methen on the arm and explained, repeating what the Rada had said.

"This is not the time for games, Jad," scolded his father.

Methen didn't find it funny either way. "Take Zua?" He looked up at the shrine. "Zua would never allow it!"

What the Rada had really said spread among them. Methen conferred with Father.

Tez's father wandered away twenty paces, looking down over the river valley below them, the route the Phentinites would likely come. Tree-covered hills of different shades of green rolled away as far as they could see. The great plain of Ren beyond, still hazed here and there with clearing mist, looked peaceful this morning.

"Quiet!" Jad's father called out, raising his arms. "Quiet! Are we forgetting?" he said, as if he had thought of a solution. "The horse lords will never let the Phentinites stay in these lands, nor stay in Ren, even if it is only to trade. They send their entire army here, all their armies, the horse lords will pin them all with a thousand arrows and leave them rotting in the sun on their sacred plains."

The Rada was looking up at him. "Boy...? Jad...?"

Jad told him what his father had said.

The Rada shook his head. "That is why the Phentinites are here in the first place," he said. "A thousand guards. One woman, the daughter of Shangar's chosen. We were her escort to the horse lords' lands, to marry her to their new king. The Phentinites will reap a thousand horses, and have free rein to travel these lands now ... mostly."

His father had seen him speaking with the Rada, and his hopeful face crumpled when Jad told him what the Rada had said, as he knew it would. His father looked to the other men with Tate, all of them gazing over the valley, trying to appear brave.

"Zua shall protect us!" Methen called out, kneeling before Zua's shrine. Masom joined him, hammer over his shoulder, and to his dismay, Jad's father trotted over too. "Zua shall guide us, shepherd us!"

In the middle of it all, the Rada lay back in the dust, loosening the binding around his leg, multiplying the black blood circles in the dust beneath him. Judging by his pale face, if he wanted to live, this should be the last he let himself lose.

Before the three ram skulls of Zua's shrine, Jad's father touched his forehead to the ground, and Jad remembered Zua's dumb, blank face. Zua would be no help to them. He couldn't even hope that he was wrong. He *knew*.

Let them take Zua, he decided, looking at his father's hands curled like hooves in the dirt. *Let them take the idiot*.

Jad stepped back. If they still needed him to repeat what the Rada said, let Tez do it. He could understand him too, even if he hadn't said so yet.

Everybody's short, squat shadows blended into blobs on the ground. His own shadow stood alone.

When he looked up, the Rada was watching him vacantly the way someone might look for shapes in the clouds.

"Jad? Jad?" A hand was shaking him. "Jad, wake up. We need to talk to you."

Jad's first thought was *The Phentinites!* He had been having fitful dreams of tall, terrifying soldiers. But as he opened his eyes and looked up into his father's calm, curious, expression, he deflated. His father's hand on his chest urged him back down onto his bedroll from where he had shot up.

The last he remembered, shovels were being hammered together, hoes and even copper axes; everyone had set to digging a trench around the village, even the littlest kids, rolling big rocks away. They would fight. *Fight for Zua!* Methen had said, and everyone gathered around to burn precious salt atop Zua's altar. Trenches would be dug; tall berms would be raised up, and if they didn't have time to build a barricade, spikes would have to do. They had set to it with vigor.

Zua will protect us!

Jad remembered Zua's wide, thoughtless face, his blank anvil eyes, and as soon as nobody needed him to talk to the Rada anymore, he had turned and practically staggered home, guided by his mother and aunt, and plonked down to sleep.

"We decided. They're bringing the Rada here," said Father. "He's only in the way in Zua's house. Bleeding all over the floor."

It took Jad a moment to push the wool out of his head. He had unraveled completely, and his father waited patiently while he knitted his thoughts together.

The sun was still shining. He couldn't have been asleep that long.

We still have time.

"Here, I brought you this," said Father, patting his crook by the bedside. "You did good, Jad, getting the flock home. And getting the Rada here to us."

There was something wrong about that. Jad's muddled thoughts wouldn't stitch together.

"Tell me about the lion," said his father.

The flock. Miu! Jad remembered like he had been slapped. *I was supposed to protect them.*

"I've never seen a lion," his father said, prompting him when he didn't say anything. "I've heard they're like cats, but bigger."

"It got Miu, and Sham," Jad said guiltily, shaking his head. *It was a monster.* Even in the daylight, home now, his thoughts condensed to dread again. He wondered if the creature had been true flesh and blood. So large, so strong and terrible, it had seemed more an evil spirit, a punishment.

Like a cat, *sort of,* he nodded. It was seven paces long, he told his father, and as tall as his shoulders. The more he told his father about its long claws, its yellowy, piercing teeth beneath its baleful eye that had stabbed a glance his way, the more he wasn't sure he was wrong.

A monster. Like one of Zua's devouring beasts. Say it. What else but a rebuke to living could such a terrible creature be? He had disobeyed his father and called the flock to the crook the way he had been told not to.

"I should have known it was there," Jad said, unable to lift his head with the shame of leaving parts of the story out.

His father clapped him on the back, and gave what was almost a little laugh. "And what would you have done if you had? Let's hope it's filling its belly on some deer up there on the mountain and leaves us alone. I don't think I could be as brave as you if I had to face it. Now, go wash the sleep out of your eyes before the men arrive."

After his nap, the late summer's pale sunshine struck Jad gently. The chirp of distant axes gave a reminder of how nothing was the same now.

He looked up from the wash bowl Miu had set out as a group of men came along the path. If he hadn't been told that the village had decided to fight, he would have known after seeing Tez's father leading the way.

Their village had no leader the way they did in Ren. The Rada's story of their big man selling his people and taking their land for himself couldn't happen here. Nobody would follow a terrible, greedy man like that. In their village, if a man proved himself good at hunting, other men would value him, follow him as a hunter. If he had a good herd, he would be valued for his advice with his animals. To try to prove that you should lead everyone in all ways was the best way to make sure nobody followed you, as nobody was expert in everything. When Tez's father said he would hunt for game near the lake, other hunters went with him. Jad was proud of how when Father decided it was time to send his flocks to the higher pastures, other flocks usually followed.

Now Tez's father had turned from hunting to war. Zua's man, Methen, had joined him, and it seemed the other men of the village were behind him.

Darson and Methen carried the Rada into their home on what looked like a ragged hammock of old fishing net, and set him down where Jad had been sleeping. The man's dark, puffy eyes stood out against his white face. Stripped of his armor, exposing his thin arms and hairy, sunken chest, he didn't look like a soldier from a proud, fearsome people, more like one of the destitute sailors who scared Jad in Ren—bitter, scowling men who lingered alongside boats loading for destinations down south; blacklisted men, his father said, maybe hoping to get home. Not cleaned or bandaged, the cut on his leg looked like a pink slice into charred steak, the spear wound on his chest a black flower.

Jad wasn't scared of this pile of rumpled cloth lying on the floor. *He's dying*, he realized, as he took his place next to his father. He had never seen anyone dying so slowly and needlessly before. After all the pain he'd suffered to bring him here, he felt … cheated.

"Tell us about the Phentinites," said Tez's father, giving the Rada a little kick.

The soldier, and everyone, looked at Jad.

"May I have some water?" the soldier said weakly when Jad translated. "I'm very thirsty."

"You may have some water when—"

Jad went outside to the water and brought back a cup for the soldier, who accepted it with trembling fingers.

"You told us about how they like to march and comb their hair," said Darson, next to Tate, "but what can we do to get them to shrink in their little dicks and turn the fuck around?"

Darson was a taller man than Tez's father but could always be found at his side. It was joked that he had bored a small hole in his house that looked out toward Tate's place so that when Tate went hunting he would be the first to follow—*Tate sends him ahead to flush out game*, was the punchline, he made so much noise. Darson laughed a lot, usually when Jad didn't know there was something funny.

"They have slingers," the Rada told them. "Only a few handfuls of them. But they're good. They will put them up high on the hill and pelt rocks down. Plunk you…" He tapped his forehead. "…right between the eyes."

"Zua will protect us," mumbled Methen, looking more confident than everyone else in the room.

To this, the Rada said nothing, and didn't look to Jad for a translation.

"The Phentinites will ask for your ... for Zua. They will take him ... back to their city, and keep him there to ensure this village stays loyal—they will want a yearly tax, probably brought to Ren."

What about the god-eating? wondered Jad. *Won't Shangar devour Zua?*

"What if we hide?" asked his father. "What if we go up into the woods, the high pastures, and wait until they leave? How long do you think they'd stay?"

The soldier shook his head. "Do you have crops? They will take them. Do you trade with Ren? They will be there. They are *staying*. If you are not here, they may not even burn the place, just move in and wait. It is nice here." He gave a strange, wan smile. "Not too hot. Not too cold. A good place to die. Whether you are Rada or you are ... you."

"How about if I drop a big shit on my floor?" laughed Darson. "Would they stay then?"

Jad didn't translate. The Rada looked up at him in that unnerving way again. "If you had a speaker, someone who could heal me ... help fend off the Phentinites—just a hint that you have a speaker—even a young one—might keep them away..."

Jad shrank, not wanting to relate what he said, remembering how Tez had exploded the last time the Rada had suggested this. But they were all looking at him, his father's steady gaze heaviest of all.

"Out with it, boy," said Tez's father.

"Probably nonsense," said Father.

"He says if we had a healer, a ... a speaker—"

"Zua will protect us!" said Methen matter-of-factly.

Tate stepped closer to the Rada. "The will of Zua will decide our fate. Not ... tricks." He kicked the soldier in the leg. "Tell us about their armor. Where are the weak spots? Where can I stab a man wearing kit like yours and the man will die the easiest?"

"If not a speaker ... I want to help," said the Rada weakly. Jad told them what he said.

Tate kicked the Rada's water cup clattering across the floor when the man reached for it. "You hate me, don't you?" he said, crouching in the Rada's face. "I can see it in your eyes. So here's your chance." Placing the butt of his spear in the man's hands, he tucked the other end against his own chest, by his heart. "Push this spear into my heart."

When Jad said nothing, "Tell him," Tez's father said, and then he barked, "Tell him, boy!"

"Tate...?" said Methen. "What are you doing?"

The Rada was looking at him anxiously, and Jad repeated what Tez's father had said.

"Do it!" said Tez's father with another kick to the soldier's leg, harder this time.

The Rada grasped the spear with his white fingers, his fingertips blood-blackened. The spear rose in his hands.

"Harder!" said Tez's father, kicking him hard in the side, with a bony thud they all heard.

Anger rippled over the Rada's face, honest and raw, his dirty teeth bared as if he couldn't hide them. It felt truer than the pleading look the man had worn until now. He pushed up off the bedroll, his thin body all knuckles, pushing up to drive the spear through Tate.

They waited, watching as a blot of blood crept down the front of Tate's shirt.

Finally, the Rada fell back, his face slackening, chest heaving.

"You want to help, fool?" said Tez's father, snatching the spear away. "You can't even stand, much less run someone through."

Tez's father shook his head. "He's useless. We can't worry

about the slingers," he said to Darson and Methen. "But we also can't defend the whole village. We'll have to cut the trench shorter, try to take away their advantage in numbers."

"Back from the hill, cutting in the shrine," said Methen as if it were obvious as they ducked out the door, Tate leading the way. "The rest of the houses are unimportant."

Father appeared to be thinking. "Jad," he said finally. "Find your mother and Miu and help them with the flock. Get them ready to move again." Then he followed Tate and the others.

Still lying on his back, the Rada had his face turned to the wall, so Jad left before the man could turn around and see him. He wasn't feeling tired anymore.

"Jad … did that man … did that man do something to you?"

Mother had dropped Moff's front hoof as she looked around and saw him. It had only been a handful of days since he had left for the high pasture with the ewes, but she looked different to him, smaller, feet hidden in the grass, the bottoms of her loose pants snagging the woodier plants.

She grabbed him, enfolding him into a big hug, warm and soft. Vaguely, he remembered feeling self-conscious of his mother's hugs. She liked to give them wherever they were, often in front of his friends, and Tez had made fun of him for it—*I wish it were my face pushing into those big mounds*, he'd say, miming pushing his face into her chest—but that seemed stupid now. Jad relaxed and hugged his mother back. It felt like it came from a good yesterday.

All the way up to this pasture, flashes of the bad dream he had been having before Father woke him pushed him along: Phentinites tall as trees in shining bronze, looming over their stakes and fences on the hill side of the village—all their village like the flock inside, pink and defenseless—the Phentinites with their smooth spears stabbing over the top at them, stabbing and laughing as if it were all good sport.

Is this my fault? he wondered. The guilt in his belly had stayed bubbling hot. After all, he had stared defiantly into Zua's awful anvil eyes. Zua, he had been told his entire life, was their protector, and Zua had cast him out of his divine meadow. Right afterward, he had returned to hear the Phentinites were coming—the timing didn't seem to be a coincidence. Maybe it was him bringing the Phentinites, responsible for what they would do—*stabbing, stabbing down...*

He swallowed hard. His chest hurt to think it. He should tell Mother what he had done. If he did, maybe Zua would not punish everyone just because of him...

Jad shook his head. *No,* he meant to say to his mother's question, the Rada hadn't done anything. He had said it all earlier before Zua's shrine. But the words wouldn't come out.

His mother rubbed the downy hair on his chin, which tickled. "He didn't ... put a spell on you ... some terrible foreign magic ... did you see him doing anything strange?"

Jad straightened, pulling back, to his embarrassment seeing two wet splotches on his mother's chest. He shook his head. "No ... Tez wanted to kill him. The Rada said he wanted to help us, and then Tez wouldn't help me carry him."

His mother frowned, as if that were only to be expected. It was the same expression she always wore when he mentioned Tez, and today it was oddly comforting. Not *everything* had changed.

She wouldn't let him pull back out of arm's reach. "Jad ... do you ... do you still trust in Zua's protection?"

No, answered his heart immediately, as he tore away from his mother's shining gaze.

There was only one thing he could say.

"Of course."

No. Zua is an idiot.

"I knew you would," she said, stroking his face, even as he remembered Zua's terrible fingers reaching for him, his awful anvil eyes. "But be careful, Jad. Follow Zua's path and don't be led astray. He will guide us through this storm, no matter what happens tomorrow. Trust in his protection."

Jad nodded, finally spotting Miu running with the flock on the other side of the meadow.

His mother brushed herself down, assuming a stern front again. "Come now," she said, "I've been waiting for you. Tell me, is there anything the matter with any of the sheep? It's a blessing you got them all home last night in the dark. Did any of them get lamed, or … hurt…?"

Together, they moved through the flock, looking for foot rot and ticks. Away from the chopping of the axes in the village, Jad heard only the bleats of the sheep and the breeze whistling through autumn's crisping grass. For a few minutes he forgot that soldiers were coming to attack their village and just helped his mother.

Jad was surprised when the flock seemed fine. If it could be called luck, having the moon had helped. Without it, he shuddered to think, likely the lion would have eaten them all.

After they had finished their quick inspection, Mother stood, hands on hips, looking pleased.

"A lot faster with two of us. You did good, Jad. I wasn't sure I wanted you fetched home, but at least it'll be easier when we move tonight, even if one of us will have to shepherd Miu too." She smiled, a joke, but when she saw him looking at her confusedly, her face fell. "Oh, your father didn't tell you, did he?" She sounded disappointed.

"Tell me what?"

"I wish he had," she sighed. "Jad, if the soldiers come and don't do anything worse than give us kisses and honey but take the sheep, we'll all still die come the winter. We have to move them … tonight."

"To the high pastures?" *The lion*, thought Jad. *Does she know about the lion?*

Mother shook her head. "There's no way out of the high pastures … if we need it. No, the meadows on the other side of the river, back under the cliffs. If we leave tonight, we can be there by late tomorrow."

"Am I…?"

"You're good with the flock. We need you, Jad, you and a few of the other boys. It'll still be dark. I guess you have experience in night herding now."

Jad turned from his mother, back toward the direction of the village. He couldn't trust that he knew what his face was doing. Father had warned him to stay away from the men building defenses. Since then, the question of what he would be doing had been sliding around in his mind. Did it make him a coward to feel relieved he wouldn't have to stand behind those stakes and face down soldiers in armor?

Phentinites stabbing, stabbing, into a killing pen.

"Jad!" his sister's small voice called out. She had followed one of that spring's ewes up underneath the trees. The last he had seen, she'd had her arms wrapped around its small neck, nose buried in its wool. "Jad, where's Miu?" she yelled, charging down through the tall grass. She kept running until she whacked her face into his belly with a hug. "I don't see her," she mumbled against his shirt.

He tried not to think of the last time he had seen the little sheep—dangling from the jaws of that monster like a mangled river rat.

His mother only shrugged when he looked to her for help.

"She … got lost," Jad said.

"You'll find her," said Miu, peeling off. "Are you coming with us?"

Jad still wasn't sure what his face was doing.

"Of course he's coming with us, dear," said his mother when he didn't answer, pulling Miu in for a half-hug. "Now go count and tell us how many ewes we have again. Maybe there's one more now. There's a good girl."

Jad watched her run off again, barely as tall herself as the sheep. So small. So delicate. She had chosen the name of her favorite ewe well.

Miu was running to me for help when the lion crushed her...

That was the moment he had understood Zua would be no shepherd to them. But he would do better. He vowed to watch over his sister Miu and see she never came to harm.

"Have you eaten anything since you got back this morning?" his mother asked. "You haven't, have you? Why don't you go on back to the house. Endo will be here soon to take watch, and I have to go speak with Beatti. Go on now. You look like you're about to blow away." With a grin, she fluttered her fingers through his hair above his ears, which had grown long enough to start feathering out and curl. "When all this is done, I'll give you a haircut."

Jad headed for home like he was told, but stopped near the edge of the trees, looking back at his mother peering into the mouth of a lamb, and at Miu hugging the little ewe that must be her new favorite. Didn't even look like one of theirs. The sun had tucked down behind the trees, casting a picket of long, swaying shadows over the meadow.

He managed to get a good five or ten minutes down the trail through the sparse trees before he had to stop, too thick with thoughts to move. All the way along the grass had kicked up the fading tartness of tall leafy plants, churned rich black dirt, the sweet scent of the dwindling summer warmth. He couldn't hold the weight in his belly down anymore. He stood there a moment, then scurried off into the bushes like he was going to throw up. Hunkered down behind a stump, he let tears fall from him onto the ferns for a few minutes until he felt empty inside. It wasn't fair. In the house he had seen his mother had been gathering berries for days, readying preserves for winter. He had been looking forward to their autumn trek to Ren when Father traded wool and cheese for salves and seeds, and salt to season the fish. Now Ren was a trap. Father's limp might have kept him from doing much pasturing himself this season, but it wouldn't keep him off the barricade tomorrow, facing down soldiers in armor.

He hated the unfair fear that squirmed through him. A nice summer night like this, normally he might find Tez and go hang out with Masom and a couple of the older boys and catch a few fish in the river. Or throw axes at butterflies. Or see who could race up what they called the climbing tree the fastest—the tall, sprawling, crumbling nearly-dead tree with branches like a ladder. Tonight the older boys were probably digging ditches or making spears, and he was out here roaming like he'd slipped away from his sleeping shepherd. He wondered if their hands were shaking like his while they sharpened stone tips and hafted them onto green-wood spears.

He couldn't stop thinking of Miu hugging that ewe. He didn't know what would happen to her while they ran from the soldiers—and make no mistake, he knew that's what they were doing. It would be worse if they didn't run. But he would make sure she was alright.

He beaded these thoughts over the ferns. Most of the way home he hid his face. Nobody would see him; they were all either digging trenches or gathering stones. He hated the stab in his chest every time he looked to the pinkening sky to see how low the sun had sunk. It was like he and everybody he knew and loved were being lowered, minute by minute, into the hot pool of tomorrow's bloody sunrise.

Jad didn't go inside his house. It looked lifeless. A chill had come down over him. It was like the approaching night had an edge he could hear rumbling ever closer. In the distance, he heard the crack of a tree splintering, and men shouting. The Rada was still inside his house. *Is he dead yet?* A pang of guilt wrung through him for half hoping he was. He closed his eyes. *Could he hear the Rada's heartbeat? Sense his warmth?* From nearby came the distinct *whump* of another tree toppling, branches crackling. He opened his eyes to see if he could spot its crown sinking below the canopy.

There was no way to tell if the Rada was dead in there from outside. That was just a child's game. And he wasn't a child anymore. He held his breath and went in.

Inside, he stepped lightly to not rattle the boards, peering at the dim lump on the floor to see if was still moving. The Rada had been left all alone.

Jad sniffed. Would he smell already if he were dead?

Then the lump moved. "Who's there?" said the Rada before Jad could step back. "Good boy? Good boy, is that you?"

Jad was standing in the bright doorway. *I don't have to answer,* he told himself. *I can just turn and leave.* He didn't owe this man, this *Phentinite*. Quite the opposite. He had saved his life, dragged him night and day from the high pastures to safety, and in return the man just lay here, in *his* bed, dying.

"What do you want?" he asked the Rada, moving to the jug where they kept some dried jerky in the cool cellar beneath the floor hatch.

"Good boy, I'm dying," said the Rada weakly, like a casual observation, his voice scratchy. It sounded odd to Jad's ear, and he nodded sharply, sarcastically, with his back turned, knowing the man likely wouldn't see.

I don't care that you're dying! he wanted to say.

"I don't want to die, good boy."

"I know!" he snapped, a short, boyish growl at the end. He was still irritated for having cried in the forest. In a way, those tears were also the Rada's fault. "You said you could help. That's why I brought you here. But you can't help! Look at you!"

Since he had last seen the Rada a few hours ago, he looked to be curling like a wet brown leaf. The man's smell hit him too, not just stale sweat and the oily musk of his clothes having dried crunchy after wallowing in the river, but the bitter blood scent of his sour meat beneath it all. He still wanted to help? By morning, the man might be little more than mulch.

"I told them everything I know," he protested, a tinge of pleading to his tone. "Everything."

Jad thought of his imagined Phentinites again. They were more real now than this man and his story of his brother or wife. *Stabbing, stabbing down into a bloody slaughter.*

"And what good will that do?" growled Jad. "Will it stop one spear? Will it make it so I don't have to leave the village tonight with all our animals? Will you stop them from killing my mother and father and my little sister?"

Jad yelled the last, breathing hard. The air had gone out of him. And his anger with it. He had said what he wanted. Mother was right: he was hungry and needed to eat; his arms ached, his bones felt wet, heavy. He had decided—he would help dig the trenches. Then he would help move the flocks to safety tonight.

But the Rada whispered, "Good boy, you could stop them…" And Jad paused.

Going back to the cellar hatch, Jad took out a small leather bag of jerky, perfect for a day's travel, or spending an evening in the forest hunting deer.

The Rada had to yell for his whispery voice to reach him across the room: "Good boy, the Phentinites would not dare threaten this village if you had a speaker. Their little snakes might turn into wiggly worms. They might be drowned in a rising river. The whole mountain might fall down on top of them. A speaker might call fire from the sky, turn their weapons to smoke. Speakers … some of them are useless fools … but some of them, good boy, some of them … let me tell you … come closer … I can't…"

Jad gave in. He came back halfway, taking a stick of jerky from the pouch and gnawing at it while the Rada looked up at him, quieter now that he didn't have to break his voice in hurling it across the room.

"A woman came to Radene once … the most beautiful woman any of us had ever seen. Dressed all in red … red hair all the way down her back to her beautiful ass. I was your age. We were having a terrible drought. Ardo wasn't listening to us—some said he had abandoned us. This woman, she named her price, and we were so hungry, so desperate … but she was no seller of healing stones and powders. My cousin was there. He said she got her money, turned around and walked out into the street. There, she called to the clouds in the sky and the rain listened and watered our land. She brought Radene back to life. Without her, the Phentinites when they came would have found an empty land of dust and rocks and great ruins scattered with the bones of dead warriors. Two months she stayed, and every day the clouds would gather. Good boy, I tell you I almost wish the Phentinites had come then. She could have demanded all of

Radene bow to her and driven away the filthy Phentinites all on her own, ruling like a queen ... but she took her coin and left, out of our land. If she were here now..."

Despite himself, growing excited, hopeful, Jad found he had to ask, "Do you know where she is? Can she help us?"

"No, good boy," the Rada said with what sounded like a short, choking laugh. "I don't know where she is. It is *you*, I mean. *You* can help us."

"I don't—"

"Good boy, you weren't afraid of that lion."

"I was..."

"Boy ... Jad ... I have looked into men's eyes as I've killed them. I've seen them..." He held his hand up to his face. "Right here. And I saw you," said the Rada, "and you weren't afraid of that lion. That beast, I have never seen anything ... it wasn't there because it wanted breakfast. It was death come for you and me and your stupid friend ... maybe just for the happiness of killing. In the dark, those green eyes turned to me and I knew then that I wouldn't die from this cut to my leg that Bonesy managed ... or this spear that idiot, Pep, drove through my shoulder. I was about to die because those eyes looked at me and I saw blood, blood ... blood. A great feast of blood that night. I saw joy for blood. But you weren't afraid ... you stopped it."

Jad shook his head. "It got little Miu. And another. Two of our flock. I was supposed to protect them and I couldn't."

Jad nearly dropped the jerky in his hand that he'd forgotten. He tucked it back in the pouch with the rest. *I should go help*, he thought. *This is heresy talk.*

"I saw what you did with your staff too. I *felt* it. Even when I thought I was going to die ... of everything I have ever seen that is strange ... good boy, I never thought I would ever see sheep moving *toward* that monster. It would be like a leaf floating upstream, or a boulder rolling up a hill. But you called them … and they came."

"I'm not supposed to do that."

"Good boy … a speaker could help…" The Rada reached out, his arm too weak to hold up, his fingers tapping the floor like a dead spider, twitching. "A speaker could heal me … easy for a speaker … and then I could help you all … your father, your mother—your little sister. Together. Good boy … don't let them find me here like this…"

Jad backed away. "I wasn't supposed to do that anymore."

"Let me face my people. Standing. In battle. The way a Rada should. I don't want to die in filth on the floor. Good boy, help me. You made the sheep turn and face the lion … help me … I know you can—"

Jad ran out the door. The light was still bright enough to blind him and he smacked hard into a pair of legs, a stiff, round belly. Big hands grabbed him and he looked up into the face of his father, dirt smeared across his cheeks and beard, purple bags beneath his eyes. He frowned and Jad tried to step back to say he was sorry, but his father held on, hands heavy on Jad's shoulders.

"Father," he said, grabbing one of his thick wrists to steady himself. "I want to help. I want to help dig the trenches and build the wall to keep the Phentinites out. I want to stay! I want to fight with you!"

The only other time Jad had seen his father look so ponderous, one of their flock had wandered off the trail and stepped into an animal hole by a log and broken its foreleg while they were traveling between pastures. It was too early in the season to simply put it down, especially as they were a day's travel from home and it would be a lot of trouble to schlep all that meat with them. But nor could they bear to see it writhing there in the meadow, hobbled, disturbing the rest of the flock with its brays of pain. Soon the wolves and eagles would be coming for it, if they weren't coming already, and they had new lambs to think of. Father had stood over the bleating animal looking much as he did now, solid like stone. Deciding, Jad thought. In the end, Father had splinted its leg the best he could with a stick, and held the heavy creature by its legs over his shoulders so it couldn't kick him all the way to the next pasturage two days' travel away.

Jad found his father's face nearly unrecognizable. There was a shadow across it, two faces layered over one another, a real one and one that struggled to stay inside.

"Why are you hiding your face, Jad?"

Jad didn't realize he had been, but he didn't want to look up either. He prayed the Rada stayed silent behind him.

"Look at me, Jad," said his father. His hands on his shoulders tightened. Father could crush shells between two fingers easily, and he felt the bones in his shoulder grind back and forth, sending a twinge down into his chest, and he made an effort to stay tall.

Jad found his father wearing the same dark, questioning expression as he had in the meadow, standing over that lamb. Then his father's face relaxed, the shadow vanishing, and to Jad it seemed like the axes in the distance grew louder; men and women were yelling sharp melodies back and forth to one another, even with the bloody clouds overhead.

"I want to help," Jad said.

Father bent down to him, kneeling in the rain-darkened dirt. "You have helped, Jad. You've helped. And you'll be helping some more tonight. If we don't hide our flocks, they'll take them, and everything our fathers and grandfathers came here to do would be for nothing."

"Then let me fight with you."

Father was shaking his head before he had even finished. "You have a more important job to do. We may die—I might die, Jad—but if you keep the animals safe, our village will stay alive. Do you understand me?"

"I don't want you to die. Your leg…"

"I don't want to die either," said Father. "But I need you to say that you understand."

Jad nodded.

"Good. Until then…" Father's hands gripped tightly again. "…don't go down to where Tate and the others are digging the trenches. Stay away from everyone. That means Tez, that means your friends. The woods too. Stay away, Jad … do you hear me?"

"But—?"

"Tell me that you'll go somewhere safe. Get some rest. You'll need it, okay? Okay, Jad? I need you to say the words."

Jad didn't understand, but he nodded again, and repeated back what his father had said.

"Trust in Zua, boy. Trust him. I gave him an offering. He's watching over us."

"Trust…" said Jad.

Inside the house, they heard the Rada coughing.

"Jad. Jad. Wake up."

His father's voice cleaved into a dream he was having about falling, falling down a black, bottomless pit. Strangely, not a terrifying dream like the dream of the Phentinites. He was plummeting down a black pit, and had been falling so long that the panic had passed, he'd had time to think on it, knowing that he had to fall properly, staying away from the sides, which looked ragged, even sharp sometimes. If he managed to do that he wouldn't be hurt; he could fall forever, as if floating. In a way, it became almost relaxing, no distraction but the wind in his robes—*robes?*—and the thoughts in his waking head finally raveling together—still, it was like a prison in a way, in that there was no way to escape, but maybe the darkness of the pit was better than the darkness he saw when he—

He sat up suddenly. *The Phentinites! Were they here?*

Again he felt his father's hand on his chest. "It's time, Jad. Time to go."

He could make out the silvery silhouette of his father crouching beneath the branches of the pine tree he had been sleeping under. The pine's needles scoured the ground of brush beneath its broad branches. Nestled against a large, old log, Jad had crawled beneath the pine into its natural, protected den. It wasn't far from the house; he came here sometimes when he wanted to be alone. Until now, he hadn't realized Father knew about it.

Darkness still filled his sleeping den, yet it was a shallower pool now, filling instead with pre-dawn's milky light. He wiped drool from his chin. There was no dew on him. So morning was coming, but the flow of it was still a trickle.

Woolly to wake as usual, Father let him gather himself, which Jad in his sleepiness found annoying. *Why is he just staring at me when the Phentinites are coming? I'm awake.*

It was as he was thinking this that his father settled himself cross-legged in beneath the pines, pushing up a large branch so that it rested tangled in his hair. He'd have little paddles of needles all through his beard, and sticky sap everywhere. But his Father looked happier, almost peaceful now compared to when he had seen him earlier. His eyes, even if still drawn down by dark bags, had settled beneath the evening's weight, and he spoke softly, contentedly, as if the two of them were sat around the fire with a pipe after a successful hunt. He saw no shadow in him now.

"Jad," his father said while Jad took a moment to wipe his eyes again, "do you trust in the will of Zua?"

His mother had asked him the same thing earlier, and just like then Jad would have said *Yes, of course*, but in his sleepy annoyance he said, "No."

He thought his father was trying not to smile. "You don't believe in the will of Zua?"

Jad remembered the broad, vengeful face of Zua lunging for him, murder in his dumb anvil eyes. Thinking of them had terrified him the past day or so, but he almost laughed now. "No," he said—distantly he could hear himself, like a petulant boy not wanting to eat his boiled roots. It wasn't a lie. He believed in Zua—more than anybody. He had *seen* Zua. Could still feel the *touch* of Zua's hard fingertips. But he had no faith that Zua cared about them.

Zua is an idiot.

His father nodded, almost as if he expected that answer. Jad weighed telling him what he really thought, about Zua in his pasture. But now wasn't the time either. He was starting to think there would never come a good time.

"Very well, Jad. Then listen well. If you don't believe in Zua's will … believe in my will. I may die today. Most of us may die today. And it is my will that you take care of your mother and Miu. I don't care how you have to do it, but don't let anything come between protecting your family and yourself. Any … any *tricks* you know … anything I don't understand yet or that you haven't been telling me … don't hold back. That is my will. Do you believe in *my* will, son?"

Jad wasn't sure he understood. "I do, Father," he said, afraid of the earnestness in his father's voice, and what he was committing to. He sensed it meant more than he knew at the moment.

"Good," said his father, holding out his hand and grasping his forearm the way two men of their village sealed their commitments. "I believe in you, Jad. You'll do what's right."

Jad didn't trust himself to speak, and embarrassed because of it, nodded solemnly. Pine needles rained on them when his father shook with quiet laughter.

Jad and his father emerged at the end of the trail where it opened up into the pasture. The large space felt like a gasp in his chest, and the dream of the pit dropped through him one last time. Father trekked on past blurry circles of ewes bundled together for warmth. The wind had settled; the night was peaceful, solemn in that way before a ceremony or sacrifice to Zua. To speak louder than a whisper would be like a rock shattering an icy puddle, never to be the same, even if it could freeze again. Low murmurs and sobs traveling far with the cool night air told them they weren't alone. Pale faces and hands moving among them were like the floating blobs he saw when he shut his eyes. Look too close and they darted away.

They came up to a mound in the grass, which rose and murmured with the voice of his mother. Still tired, not wanting to speak, the more he searched the more people he spied in the dark. Who would be coming with them? Who was out there?

"No, don't wake her," he heard Father say, he guessed of Miu, probably sleeping among the sheep. "The less she knows of what's going on, the better."

"You get some sleep, Jad?" his mother asked. He turned to see her facing his way, and he nodded and said he did.

"I found him having some peaceful dream," said Father.

One at a time, out of the gloom shadows of men began loping across the pasture back toward the village. Jad got a tight

[77]

feeling in his chest to see how they moved alone, as if unaware there were more of them all drifting in the same direction.

Zua drawing them close with his golden crook.

Father looked up at the sky. Blue smeared the black on the horizon.

Jad nearly jumped when Father's hand fell on his shoulder. "You remember what I said, don't you, Jad? Whatever you have to do…"

Jad looked out over the blurs of sheep. He knew he was a good shepherd. "I do," he said.

Women's voices traveled from the other side of the pasture, already clicking and calling for their flocks. The first dog barked. His father patted him on the shoulder before starting down the slope back the way they had come. *Drawing him close.* One more dark figure losing form as he floated toward the path in the woods.

Jad felt like he should follow him. He waited, and he didn't move.

Mother called for all their sheep to wake.

All around them, the flock stood.

Walking with his mother and Miu, keeping the flock between them, it could have been any morning moving pasturage. Only that there was a sense of urgency today, and they were with other flocks, other families, made it different. Between them, the flock didn't care. Little Miu plucked blank faces of flowers from moonlit gaps between the trees and put them in her hair, then found her friend Suba with her family and ran back and forth in the darkness with her.

It bothered Jad, if only a little, that they were last to leave the pasture, and thus the last in the procession. Normally it was Father and him leading. Mother hadn't said a word since Father had left. Sleepiness blanketed her shoulders. Jad could see her doing her best to keep the worry from her face and offer a smile whenever Miu bounced near with small fistfuls of wilty white petals for her.

Jad lost track of time as they led the flock up and down through a few shallow valleys and across trickles of water that in the early summer would be impassable torrents of mountain runoff—there were hundreds of them in these hills—and then into another broad plateau of grass and small trees gnarled by winter winds. In a pinch, sometimes they brought their flock here to graze. In summer there were few bugs, but little protection from the biting wind either.

As the cool morning breeze began to flow down from the

high horizons, in the distance Jad thought he could see the sharp, sheer cliff they would be aiming for, like a white face waiting for them in the gloom. The pastures beneath it were broad, surrounded by trees, and thus protected from the worst gales, if not from some of the huge rocks tumbling from the cliffs above, which sometimes came crashing like wrath through the treetops and grumbling out onto the grassy plateau. That was why they only relocated their flocks there as a last resort.

Jad looked back often. The twisting shadows of trees and the spattering of stars above stayed unchanged. He kept wondering how the day would go. *Battle.* Mother said there was a chance there wouldn't be a battle, *slaughter*, which fell in line with what the Rada had told them. Maybe they would decide to give some of the spring lambs to Ren every year, or a supply of fish from the river. It was possible, she said, that later today they might look up to see Father crossing the pasture to fetch them and tell them all about it. The more she talked, the more hope wormed into her.

Jad tried not to think about it. He looked ahead over the column of mothers and sheep and children, sharper than just dim shapes in the darkness now. Nothing could stop the dawn from coming. He could finally make out the bobbing, swaying horns of the skulls mounted on Zua's shrine, strapped to the back of a sledge being hauled by two rams up ahead, leading them away.

The Phentinites would ask for boys, for men, to fight for them, and demand they give over the skulls from the shrine of Zua to ensure those promised boys, and lambs, and fish reached Ren every spring. Tate, and Methen, and Father, they would never give up Zua. Without him, their village wouldn't exist. They would fight. Father wouldn't be showing up with good news at the pasture. *When they're finished in the village, the soldiers will come looking for us to take the skulls. And the boys. And the girls. And the women. They'll find the old men who had hidden in the hills.*

A child could follow the path made by forty people and two hundred sheep crossing a grassy plain.

Maybe that was why his mother was talking so much.

"Mama, I'm tired," whined Miu, swishing a stick back and forth, whipping the heads from dandelions. The newness, the sense of fun, had begun to wane.

"We're almost there, my little lamb," said Mother. A fib. They wouldn't reach the pasture until at least midafternoon, when the sun was high and whatever was about to happen in the village would long be finished. It mollified Miu, who trusted them. For a while she strutted along with long steps, arms flopping by her side, until she forgot to be tired and went to find Suba again. It used to be that she and Endo could entertain each other for a while too, but Jad had spotted Endo farther ahead, still corralling the rams, with their dog Pusher trotting alongside. After the fray of dragging the Rada back to the village yesterday, Jad had spied his cousin off to the side, hugging his arms around the dog's neck, and the dog licking his face happily.

After a while, Jad fell back to make sure they weren't losing strays in the darkness, and so Mother could settle some with Miu half hanging off her hand. He kept losing ground anyway, always stopping to look behind. It might have been the lightening sky he was guarding against.

As they were nearly across the long plateau, word came filtering back that they would stop soon to take some water and let the animals rest before they descended into the next valley. There was a wide river to cross there, flat and shallow this time of the summer like the rest, but every crossing had its challenges. That's when Jad looked up and saw someone standing by the side of the column, short, round, and it wasn't a crook he was holding in his hand like he and so many others held.

"Tez!" he called out, waving, surprised to see him. He hadn't

talked to him since they'd brought the Rada home. He'd
thought for sure Tez would be fighting with the men. In a way,
soldiers attacking their village was the fulfillment of every one
of his dreams; he finally had the chance to prove himself. But
perhaps Tez's father, like his, had tasked him with
protecting...?

No, Tez's mother was dead, no brothers or sisters, and
precious few sheep.

Whatever the reason, resentment for being here was
probably burning a hole right through him, Jad thought—half-
deliciously.

"Hi, Tez," he said when he came closer. It felt like the first
time he'd been happy to see him in a long time. Being together
at the start of the past awful couple of days, that meant
something.

Tez planted himself like the scowling stump of a broken
tree. "I should have been watching you more closely. I thought
you were in the front, not back here where you can sneak off.
Too late for you now. I see you."

Jad laughed. "What are you doing here? Protecting us all?"
After Jad's nightmare of giant Phentinite soldiers stabbing,
stabbing, little Tez looked like he was hanging from his spear,
not holding it.

"I told you," Tez growled. "I'm watching *you*! Spy!" he spat,
and jabbed Jad in the shoulder with the butt end of his spear.

It hurt, and Jad stumbled, rubbing away the pain. It was rare
for the flocks to be moving all at once, and all morning the
families had been helping one another, corralling strays,
including rounding up the children. He had been enjoying it as
the one bright pinprick in a gloomy morning, so of course Tez
had to do what he always did and darken it with his anger and
stupidity.

On second thought, Jad didn't want to deal with Tez right
now.

Why can't we just be in this together?

Ignoring the pain in his shoulder, he kept following Mother and the flock. He was in danger of becoming the stray.

Tez followed directly behind him so that Jad had to walk backwards to see him. "I thought you'd be fighting," he said, hoping it stung Tez a little. "Father asked me to take care of my mother and Miu and our flock."

"Liar," said Tez. "They wanted you to leave so you couldn't do something bad when the Phentinites attacked, some foreign heretic trick!"

Too tired to argue, Jad gave a short chuckle.

But Tez went on: "Sent you away with the women so they could be sure. But my father and Methen, they told me to follow you, and if you tried to do some Phentinite spells…"

It was the sour, hateful look on Tez's face that made him realize his friend wasn't joking.

"…if you tried to come back, or do any of your foreign magic, they told me to kill you."

Jad laughed again, differently than when he'd laughed a moment ago, when it had been real. "That's stupid, Tez," he said with a shrug.

In the back of his mind it twigged at something his father had told him that morning. He had been so sleepy, trying to listen…

Jad stopped walking. He was tired of Tez being stupid. Now was not the time. "Tez … that's not funny." You always had to kick Tez's awful jokes back to him or else he might keep repeating them.

Tez halted behind him and raised his spear. "Then why do you speak their language?"

"You did too!"

Tez's face puffed like he had been punched in the belly. "You did first! You made me! You used one of your foreign spells! That's what my father said!"

"Tez…"

The column slowly moving away, Jad saw his mother look back and squint at them—*He's just talking with Tez*. She lingered a moment, bent to Miu, and continued on. Now Jad really did feel like a stray.

This is stupid, he thought again. He trotted after her to keep up. Tez, behind him, kept pace. It annoyed Jad having him back there, clutching his useless, too-long, too-heavy spear. Tez could barely thrust it properly—like Jad had heard his mother say, he would probably never grow into it. He took after his dead mother, who was short and stout.

What was it Father had said to him this morning? He couldn't *think* with Tez back there.

"Stop following me," he said over his shoulder.

"No! I have to watch you … traitor."

Anger had been simmering in Jad all morning, and now it boiled over. Before he could stop himself, he spun, and wrenching his crook up, jabbed the rounded end smack into Tez's face—a solid bop like braining a fish on a rock.

He pulled back at the last moment, but Tez couldn't have been watching him very closely, as he walked right into it with a sharp *braugh!*—a bray almost like a sheep getting a headbutt to the flanks. He collapsed in a heap, grabbing at his chin.

Jad stepped back, huffing like a bellows with the anger that still burned in his arms but knowing better than to stand over Tez when he was mad.

For being short and round, Tez could move quickly when he wanted. He leapt up, his spear clutched in both hands, and charged straight at him like he wanted to run through him. Jad barely had time to sidestep as Tez lunged, and a searing jolt shot through him—he felt the spear bite hard against his stomach.

That's when he knew, no doubt now, this was real. Tez had come at him with his spear before, swinging it like a club, nudging him with the butt end, but he had just sidestepped a killing blow. Tez hadn't hesitated. He had tried to skewer him.

Before Tez could rear back and thrust again, Jad knocked his spear down with his crook, keeping it there, kicking awkwardly at Tez to get distance.

They told me to kill you, he heard Tez say in his mind. He hadn't wanted to believe it.

But it didn't matter what he believed. Tez's face told him it was true. It was the last look that many a falling leaf and fish and squirrel had seen—Tez's puffy cheeks folded up with hate gave him a round-faced, moony look that Jad had once found funny, and it made him laugh again now, just a quick, rude, bark. There was nothing Tez hated more than being laughed at. Times Jad wanted Tez to be mad, he found some way to laugh at him, and this time was no different.

Tez lunged at him again.

They told me to kill you.

In a way, it *was* funny, as he had spent the last two days thinking the worst possible thing had happened. It was the end of their village and his people. Their houses might burn. They might be captured as slaves. Father might die. And all along it had been worse than he thought.

Jad was taller and had leverage. He dropped his crook, pushing Tez's spear down as he thrust again. Tez, though, had more weight and all the momentum. Anger had always been the stone rolling inside of him. He grunted, digging in and shoving back.

Then Tez surprised him. He let go of the spear. It was like a wolf dropping its teeth, or a turtle shedding its shell. Jad couldn't get his hands up before Tez crashed into him, driving him onto his back in the tall grass and falling on top of him, landing a knee into his belly. Breath whooshed out of Jad, the two of them tangled like branches in the wind. The tall, stiff grass scratched his eyes as Tez's fists smacked down clumsily, his friend's eyes and nose and mouth contorted like a face in the knots of a tree.

Jad couldn't get his hands up to stop a hollow-sounding blow to his cheek.

They told me to kill you.

Where was Mother? Miu? Beatti? Was anyone back there to see them?

They told me to kill you.

Would anyone care if they did see, or would they just see two boys tussling in the grass and move on?

The same sort of hate that he could see in Tez's face rose up in him. *Lies.* After all he had done to help, everything he had been told the past day had been lies. He pushed against Tez, punching back. He didn't care where he hit as long as he hurt Tez.

But it was too late. It didn't matter. Punches rained down, thumping his forehead, his cheeks. He couldn't stop them all, and with his head against the hard, dry ground, each blow boomed through his skull. His hands squished into Tez's chest; he heaved up, finding Tez wasn't moving. *Too heavy.* And taking the time to push gave Tez chances to land solid punches to his face. He heard a crunch. Lights flashed in his eyes.

I can't get him off, he realized, unable to get a full breath. Can't push him off or get a hard punch.

It was unfair. Useless tears of rage rolled back into his hair.

He wished Tez weren't so stupid.

Wished he had stayed to fight with the rest of the men.

Died with them.

There was a pause in the punches. He forced his eyes open, which had narrowed to slits whipped at by the sharp knots of grass. Had Tez stopped?

No.

Tez hefted up a stone the size of two fists.

They told me to kill you.

Jad grabbed for Tez's arm, but it was like grasping a snake's skin.

...*to kill you*...

The idea drained his strength. It was only by luck that his elbow struck down on the top of his gnarled crook lying in the grass next to them.

Tez lifted the rock high, and Jad wrenched the crook's tip up into Tez's chin. It was a bent, sloppy blow, not strong. He saw it almost in slow motion, how Tez's teeth snapped out of joint for a second—the way a knapped rock suddenly cleaves. It was enough to knock Tez back.

Tez's eye found his. They rarely met eyes. For a moment, some sense of reason came back to Tez's face. A thinking expression behind the surprise.

They had tussled, wrestling, face to face, on hundreds of occasions. They would still walk home together, if ruefully. That was just what friends did. That was just Tez, cruel and stupid. Now Jad saw that thinking face sliding away like mud into a stream, and there was no recognition of them being friends left behind. More it was like the vicious gleam he'd seen dozens of times in Tez when he had stabbed some small creature with his spear, or pinned a bird out of the air for fun with a stone. Tez's lips pulled back, his yellowy teeth bared.

The shared moment lasted a single thud of the thumping in Jad's head. He didn't hesitate. He swung the crook up again, smacking hard against Tez's temple with a solid, hollow *thok*, like kicking a rotted log.

Tez's yellowy teeth disappeared behind his lips.

Jad drew back. *Thok*. And again. *Thok*.

Tez tottered, the look of shock on his face almost funny, and Jad took the opportunity to swing the crook back two-handed, with strength. The fourth strike, Tez's head snapped back and he toppled off to the side.

The dim, grassy field spun as Jad pushed out from under

Tez's heaviness. His friend's spear lay at his feet. He scooped it up before Tez could bowl into him, and turned brandishing both the spear and his crook.

Tez was wobbling to push upright, eyes unfocused, lips twisted.

I could kill him right now, Jad thought. There was power in that. His limbs sturdied again. Breath brought purpose. *Is he going to keep chasing me? What will he say to the others?* The pain filling Jad's head flared over into anger. *What has he already said? To Mother? To Miu?*

In the grass he saw the stone Tez was going to hit him with—jagged and dense. It would have turned his head to porridge.

He dropped his crook. It was only by luck that he was alive to have this choice. *Tez tried to kill me.* It would only be fair. Tez didn't give him the same courtesy.

Blood ran down the side of his friend's face, his chin and eye swelling.

"Give me my spear," said Tez, holding his hand out.

Jad blinked. Right then, nothing else could have made him laugh, but he couldn't stop himself, couldn't stop it from coughing up out of him, cruel and slow and delicious.

"No," he said when he could talk. His lip felt strange—fat, or split.

Tez screamed at him. "GIVE ME BACK MY SPEAR! PHENTINITE!" His voice cracked, scratchy like a toddler's. "GIVE IT BACK. IT'S MINE!"

He lurched forward unsteadily. Jad stepped back, brandishing Tez's own spear at him. "I'll run you through, Tez. I'll do it!"

"It's mine!"

"Don't move. I'll kill you, Tez."

Jad tightened his grip on the spear, shocked to discover he meant it. If he had to, he would drive the spear through his friend. He would kill him.

Tez weaved to a wind only he could feel. Without his spear, it looked like part of him was missing.

A bird without wings, a fish without a tail.

Just a boy who threw rocks at sheep when Tate wouldn't take him hunting as he couldn't sit quietly.

"You're weak," sneered Tez. "You can't do anything. You can't hurt us. You're too weak!"

This sounded like the old Tez.

He thought about what Tez had said, about Tate and Methen saying he should kill him if he needed to, and it came to his mind that what he had been trying to remember was that it was his own father who had told him to do whatever he had to do to protect his mother and Miu.

Is Tez a threat to Mother and Miu?

His hands urged him to decide: keep this annoyance in front of him or sweep it away? This thought came to him like a sturdy rock in the middle of a river's torrent.

Tez backed up. "Weak! You're weak!" he yelled, eyes scrunched. "I'm going to go where they really need me! I'm going to go help kill your *friends!*"

To Jad's surprise, Tez turned and ran, and never once looked back, shrinking smaller, smaller, as he trampled along the tattered path between the almost spectral curtains of morning mist. In the dim light of dawn, it didn't take long before the dot of him running dissolved into the gray distance.

Tez was gone. Jad watched him go. Then dropped the tall spear into the cage of the high grass.

He hadn't made a decision about Tez. Some part of him *tsked* in disappointment.

The birds hiding, the trees holding back a shiver, the dim plain had grown quiet, as if judging. He turned and saw that the flocks and the families of his village had moved on without him. He was alone. *Strayed.*

Blood tickling his chin, he wiped at it, his face numb, feeling twice the size it should. His head throbbed, as did all his fingers, yet his yellowy knuckles sang out their scrapes the loudest.

I almost died. Feeling thin, hungry, scared, sad, he lowered himself to one knee, then both, eye-level in the grass. Just to rest for a minute. *Tez almost killed me.*

Clean golden light then shot across the tops of the mountains, brightening the mist above him a brilliant white. The morning had come.

This summer, with Father's injury, while tending their flock Jad had spent days sleeping beneath a blanket of clouds, listening to the chorus of owls and bats and animals in the trees, the mountain wind's howling high above. He had liked it. He had felt important, like he was helping. But until now, looking down at the mangle of grass where he had fought Tez, he had never felt *alone*.

The air had stilled as if spooked, yet ahead the grass blurred into a pale green wave that beckoned him forward. Dawn's light was oozing over the tops of the far, low hills, their feet still shrouded in night's shadow. Jad blinked forcefully, urging himself to walk faster despite the wobble in his step, the throbbing in his head, the blood beating, *beating*, his desire to catch up catch up with his mother and the rest of the village.

Strayed.

All day he had been told different things, and now he knew some of those things were lies. *Tricks.* How his father had said the word ran through his mind. Not just *Protect your mother and Miu*, his father had said any *tricks* you know, don't hold back. The word *tricks* hissed up from the whispering of the dry autumn grass and blurred out into the mist.

There was an echo of *tricks* in how Tez had told him: *If you tried to come back, or do any of your foreign magic, they told me to kill you.*

Foreign magic? Did Father think he was a Phentinite spy too?

No, of course not. But it reminded him of all the things the Rada had told him that afternoon. *Good boy, you could stop them. Good boy, you weren't afraid of that lion.*

In his fatigue, and his desire to get clear of the man, he had practically forgotten, especially as he *had* been afraid of that lion. At the time, he just had a sense, as silly as it sounded, that it might … listen.

Tricks.

Had Father been eavesdropping on him speaking with the Rada?

The low rise between here and the river was enough to hide the flocks, but grass forty paces wide had been trampled flat. Obviously they had come this way.

Everything would be alright. He would be safe again when he caught up with his mother. Maybe he could help carry little Miu for a while, or play with her, distract her, pick flowers.

A fight with Tez. That's what he would tell Mother had happened to his face.

That was one easy. Too true, and too frequent.

The land rolled like a boat when he tripped on a lump in the grass. He hadn't been watching, distracted by the Rada's voice in the thumping of his head: *Good boy, you could stop them … stop them…*

Topping a low rise a couple minutes later, white blurs of sheep's ears were flicking in the green ahead. The flocks had come farther than he had expected, spreading out to graze at the thinning edge of the mountain meadow, where the pasture grew sparser, dotted with small bushes, more like a rocky promontory with thistles and scratchy grass. Already he was passing a few strays who had found precious grass to nibble and lingered behind. The dark wall of the rest of the flock, and the people with them, were resting where the grass met the trees ahead.

Tricks. The only *trick* he had ever shown Father was how he could call the sheep with his crook.

For the first time, Jad wondered if that wasn't normal. *Didn't the sheep came to the crook? Couldn't everybody do it if they wanted, if it weren't forbidden?* So many things were forbidden, either by Father or Zua, he hadn't thought much about it.

Jad stopped and wiped at a tickle on his face, surprised to find his cheeks wet.

If it wasn't the crook … could he do that *trick* without it? Was that the kind of thing the Rada had been talking about? *Good boy*, he remembered him saying, *I tell you I almost wish the Phentinites had come then. She could have demanded all of Radene bow to her, and driven away the filthy Phentinites all on her own…*

Maybe the speaker woman the Rada had told him about would have driven them away the same way he had called the sheep … except the opposite…

Jad stopped, spotting his mother speaking with Aunt Beatti, Miu half asleep hanging from her hand like a dangling leaf. If he was going to try this, his *trick*, to see if he could do it without Father's crook, he should do it here, before Mother or anybody else saw him.

He counted the strays surrounding him. He'd call them together into a ten-paces circle, same as he had the other day in the high mountain meadow. If they came … then maybe the Rada was right, and more than just running away with the flocks, he could help send the invaders away.

Chilly now that the dew was settling and soaking in, he put his crook down in the grass and huffed on his fingertips to warm them. Normally, he would jam the crook down and yell for the sheep to come to him, but here he would have to try it quietly.

He stayed low. Nobody had seen him yet.

Stretching hurt, breathing hurt. He nudged the thick top of the crook away with his foot, drank a long breath, clenched his fists, reached as tall as he could, *a quick test*, and swung his hands down in the same planting motion he would make if he were still gripping the crook.

He had meant to sneak...

Meant to do what his mother needed him to do...

What Father said he should do...

But at the last moment, alone, terribly alone in the scrubby meadow with his thoughts...

Mother and Miu having to leave home, sleeping in the grass, that sadness burning in his throat...

Father with his twisted knee, his limp slowing him all summer, tall soldiers spearing him...

Tate and Methen and Masom and everybody in the village he'd known his whole life casting evil looks at him as if he were a stranger...

The lying Rada who could help, gabbling nonsense...

Everything unfair since he had offended Zua by the gorge...

All the boiling, ugly, violent, anger he'd been holding back all night and for days ... swung down in his fists.

They told me to kill you.

In his mind he didn't whisper the words. With rage he crunched them tight and burned them instead.

COME TO ME!

Jad had once seen lightning blast a tree at the edge of a pasture—the very pasture they were heading for today. It had been late in the summer. Father had been having some dispute with Methen over what Zua wanted them to trade for in Ren. He'd wanted to get away. *To settle my mind*, Father had said before they set out. The sky had clouded; Jad had sensed the tingle of power on the nape of his neck. First, a loud crack had split the air. Then Father pointed up at the trail of smoke rising from the tree line. Not a second later there was another crack; the whole top of a tree forked with blue flame all at once. Jad remembered it as the first time he had ever said a swear word in front of Father and Father hadn't said anything, too rapt in watching the tree explode. The grass, Jad had reflected later, had rippled for a hundred paces around, crowned with tiny wisps of smoke. The sheep had turned and run, terrified, just as with the second *crack* both he and Father had stumbled, and Jad had felt the power of the strike fizzing in the ground and washing over him, and in the air he breathed...

As his fists slammed to a halt, *COME TO ME!* his hot clenched anger raced out rumbling between all the millions of stalks of grass, the air shimmering like the sky itself had drawn a breath, and Jad was reminded of the fear and the power of that day.

There was a moment of calm. Then he heard the birds.

Morning having crept down from the peak of the hills, dawn's fresh glow had covered the wide plain, and from all bright corners of it a black fog was rising to darken the sky again. Birds were shooting into the air—the thousands of small, agile birds that lived in the grass and fluttered up with one's passing, and from the farthest tree line a pulsing of large black birds billowing up like smoke. All around, without a chirp or squawk, the beating of their uncountable wings fluttering all together hushed like the silencing roar of a waterfall, flattening the meadow with the push of their passing as they boiled into the air.

Jad shrank down as their shadow passed over him, the river of birds winding in a smooth, surging, mass, blocking the sun. The plain grew like night again, until with horror Jad realized they were veering nearer, circling tighter and tighter in a dark whorl right above him.

A sheep lowed cheerily behind him. The nearest small group of five that had been grazing on tough, spindly tufts were gazing at him dumbly, as if waiting for him to tell them what to do next. He had called them. *It worked.* Even without the crook.

He didn't know how to feel about that. Like black rain, small birds began alighting all around him, bending the tips of the tall, bushy-headed grass and covering the sheep's backs, first only a few, then dozens, then hundreds, swooping in like storm-blown leaves, their quick colorless eyes striking all over him.

Oh no…

Worse, when he looked around, beyond the birds hundreds more sheep with their dumb anvil eyes were stepping his way slowly, contentedly—*all of them*. All the flocks of the village.

He swore, ducking lower. Of course with all the sheep moving in the same direction, everyone had stood from where they were resting, wondering where they were going.

So much for staying secret. He might as well have been dancing there blowing a horn. He had only wanted to help. Now they were all going to be angry with him.

He peeped up, looking for Mother and Miu, and saw them standing too. His mother looked sad, and like everyone else, confused.

Protect your mother and Miu, his father had said. This wasn't that.

They were coming. And not just them—*everyone*—following to collect the sheep, which were now moving the wrong way.

He swore again, and slowly he stood, accepting there'd be no hiding for him. How could he explain this? Surely he couldn't say it was the will of Zua. Nobody would believe him.

After Tez … he knew.

But something was wrong. Except for the steady crackling of all the hundreds of sheep approaching through the stiff grass as if sleepwalking, and the plapping of descending birds flapping their little wings all around him, nobody was calling out, not to their sheep, not to each other. Like the birds, nobody was making a sound.

His mother's face looked strained, as if in pain, and at her side little Miu's face screwed up with sobbing. Yet she, and everyone else, kept the same unhurried step toward him.

Like a slap it struck him: *I called them. Not just the sheep and the birds, but everyone. I called them.*

Movement by his feet caught his attention. Beetles and worms and crickets and centipedes were crawling up out of the brush in a writhing tangle.

Oh no… stop this. Stop! Stop! he thought.

Following the smaller birds, the big crows and the ravens, and even a few hawks and big, killing birds, talons extended to land, were swooping down in a circle like an eddy of black smoke all around him. Jad clapped his hands over his ears as a great chaotic chorus erupted from them now with his plea, the thousands of birds exploding in all directions screeching and twittering.

At the same time, like marionettes having their strings cut, all of his people slumped. The tips of the grass across the plain rustled, and a collective worried *baaaa* went up among the sheep. Jad's mother turned to comfort little Miu—everyone was looking to their neighbors, befuddled, helping one another. A few of the elders had fallen.

Jad's mother was the only one who never turned away for a second.

Jad grabbed up his crook and retreated back through the battered remains of the tall grass, bugs raining over his legs and crunching underfoot. Above, the cloud of black birds were shattering in all directions, a torrent of tweets and chirps and squawks breaking apart in the sky, feathers raining down, and he ran through the expanding flashes of their shadows shivering all around him.

Jad's long crisp shadow tangled through the autumn brush and wavered through the streams. It was by a low, pebbly brook that he stopped, the overhanging trees erasing the dawn's light and his long, traveling shadow with it. His legs wouldn't move, locked halfway between running away and running toward.

Itchy all down his arms, he bent to douse his hands in the cold water, numbing his fingers. As cold as they were, he still felt the filth of what he had done. Mother's expression ran with him, the sorrow and fear he saw there ... he didn't know what he had done, only that it would surely be against Zua's will. He couldn't go back.

Ahead, then? To the village. Could he help? *Is this what Father wanted?*

He didn't think so.

The Rada. He might know.

If it wasn't too late.

He was right. If the Phentinites had wanted to follow the flocks, their path from the village was obvious. Even through the hardier brush, with the broken branches and sheep spoor they could follow practically by touch and smell.

At a run, getting all the way back felt like no time at all, and he found his house quiet. Without thinking on it, he was listening for the sounds of clashing metal, of men yelling. If there were no screams in the distance, he also heard no axes chopping, no chuff of shovels. From inside, though, he thought he heard the sharp edges of voices, and crept into the dimness.

"Good boy," he heard the Rada say, weakly, if still welcoming.

It took a few moments for his eyes to adjust. The smell of meat had grown pungent in the room.

"Come to help your friends, traitor?" spat Tez.

Jad stepped back, blinking away the red blobs in his eyes, until he could see Tez standing above the Rada's bed, holding another spear he had gathered from somewhere with both hands, ready to stab down.

"Good boy ... you have come to help," the Rada said, nearly as a whisper, his eyes like two wet holes in soft ground. The rest of him looked as fragile as a cracked egg, his coarse face painted on.

Jad studied Tez's moving expression. He looked happy to see Jad too.

"Stay over there," said Tez. "I'll deal with you in a minute."

The Rada beckoned toward Jad. "You want ... you want to help drive off those Phentinite pigs..."

"Look at me!" yelled Tez, bending over the Rada, threatening to bring the spear down. "Look at *me*! Look at me while you die!"

The Rada seemed to have no care for the spear tip wavering just inches above his belly. "My fellow Rada who conquer in the name of those Phentinite pigs," he said, still looking at Jad, "they don't deserve to be called Rada. I will h—"

"Stop talking to him! Look at me!" yelled Tez, raising the spear, meaning to drive it down—and then drive it down again and again, the way Jad had sometimes seen him hack at rolls of wool bundled for sale—*A bundle of wool takes about the same amount of pressure as a man*, he'd say.

Face red, Tez kicked the Rada in the side, forgetting the spear for a moment. The Rada grunted, but unlike when Tate had kicked him, the Rada took the blow, leaned back and laughed, if only managing a trickle of it. This brought a second kick from Tez, as Jad knew it would, and for the first time since he had entered the room, the Rada rolled his head up and looked Tez full in the face, shaking with mumbled laughter still.

"Did you say something, little squirrel?"

Tez gritted his teeth, and raised his spear high, but Tez never got the chance to bring it down. Jad didn't see where the Rada had concealed the knife. It just came swinging out toward Tez's leg while his spear was drawn up above his shoulders, poised awkwardly.

Tez chirped, high and throatily, and toppled into a heap.

The Rada wasn't fast. The rot had got all through him. But Tez had fallen close and the Rada didn't need to be fast, only deliberate and efficient. Two hands on the small knife, he buried it into Tez's belly, stopping him yelling about how his ankle hurt.

Tez grunted like he had simply stumbled—then the Rada tugged the knife up like a lever, holding it there a few seconds before jabbing again, higher this time as he was falling back onto his bedroll. The third stab, less precise, made a hard click of bone into Tez's cheek.

Finally, the Rada lay back panting, knife clutched to his skinny shoulder. Two breaths and it was over. Tez stopped moving. He had barely made a sound.

"Tez?"

It felt like the sun fell and rose again in the time it took Jad to shuffle across the floor to his friend's side. He shook his shoulder as if to wake him, finding him loose, heavy, his lips slack, hinges of crusty black blood between his teeth from when he had knocked him in the face with his crook in the clearing. Tears tickled the back of his hand. *Tez would be mad to have my tears on his arm.* This, too, seemed unfair. Warmth on his knees, Jad looked down. Tez's blood, thick and acrid, the same as any sheep or goat his father had ever slaughtered, was pooling out beneath him.

You would have thrown up, he heard Tez say. *The blood ran like this...*

But Tez was wrong, the way he knew he would be. *You're wrong, Tez!* He didn't feel like throwing up. He wanted Tez to not be dead. Then he could finally show him he wasn't sick. "Tez!"

He had no fear of the Rada next to him, whose heavy gasps rattled like pebbles on a wave-washed shore. Another minute and the man might blacken and sprout mushrooms.

"Tez! Come back! Tez!"

Laying both hands on Tez's shoulders, he gripped hard and listened. For what he wasn't sure. Not words. Not breath. From somewhere distant, separate from the ringing silence in his ears and the warmth on his knees, a great blank came over his mind, the absence in the hum of the world that now he realized he had been hearing his whole life, the muttering of the trees and the grass and the mountains telling him what they were. It felt like denial, knelling as loud as any bell. He drew a shuddering breath like he'd been punched in the chest. Tez was gone.

"He was going to kill me," whispered the Rada. "I had to. He would have been sloppy."

Tez's face had slackened into a peace Jad had rarely seen on him, even with the flap of skin hanging from beneath his cheek. This peaceful boy didn't look like Tez.

"Good boy," whispered the Rada next to him, half breathless, "I heard my people pounding shields a few minutes ago. They will bash shields … to scare the enemy … or to cover the noise of the others sneaking around … to the rear…"

I should find Father, thought Jad. *Help him. Fight with him.* That was the right thing to do. That's what Tez had meant to do before this outsider had killed him.

Zua's beasts will eat the Phentinite soldiers. They will be devoured in his dark forest.

The Rada's hand with Tez's blood smeared over it, drying to black already, landed on his arm. "Good boy … the woman … the speaker who came to Rada … she healed many … many men the maidens of death were dragging over the battle lines…"

Jad hardly heard him. While he was speaking, a chorus of angry voices sang out, a short, sharp, yelp, he assumed from outside the village, quickly followed by a man shouting, too far away to discern what was being said.

Jad looked up at the Rada. The man's face had tightened with pain, desperation, and the strain of trying not to show it. The bones of his cheeks cast a shadow over his lips, which were pulled back with thirst—a face Jad might see poking up out of a small hole in the plains.

"Phentinite pigs," the Rada whispered, yellowy teeth showing. "You are … good boy. Good … Jad. I can … help."

More angry voices called out in the village. Tez's blood was creeping beneath the Rada. Then, *Father!* Jad heard the voice of his father answering—angrily—small and far away, but a son recognizes his father's voice. It drove an icicle down through him.

Jad stood, stepping over Tez and the Rada to kneel on the other side where he wouldn't be getting his knees bloodied.

He believed the soldier. The man wanted to help. The hate on his face, it could be trusted.

"How do I do it?" Jad asked. "How do I … how do I help?"

"I…" The Rada's shoulders settled onto the mat. "I do not know. Speak it…" he said quietly, nearly a question.

Tez's eyes stared blankly at the floor. Jad reached over and closed them, and leaned back with blood on his hands, which he wiped on the Rada's shirt.

Any tricks you know, his father said. It would have to be a good trick.

It pained him to remember calling the sheep to him in the meadow, how his mother had looked at him with dismay … but that had worked. Could that stop the Rada from dying?

Eyes closed, he raised his hands high, then brought them down again above the Rada. *Make him better!* he thought.

The Rada's black eyes roamed around the room. *Nothing happened.* When he had called to the sheep, it had been so easy, so clear…

All those hundreds of sheep peering at him with their dumb, anvil irises, and all his people seeing him, staring, unblinking…

Tez's eyelids had slid back, staring half-lidded, empty, catching the reflection of the door so that it looked like a light shone out of his head.

They told me to kill you.

In frustration, Jad grabbed fistfuls of his hair. It wasn't fair.

None of this. *It worked before!* He clenched his fists until his nails made bloody dents in his palms, resisting the urge to pound them down onto the soldier.

It was looking down at the Rada that he saw the man had changed, and what he saw scared him. *What is this?*

More than the man lay beneath him. Too much to take in all at once. It was like he had pulled back five paces inside his head, looking out, and he saw how the man before him—not just a collection of bones and meat and blood—was also all his choices sketching his path from his faraway home to here, connections shooting wide and far across the land. He lay over the skin of the world as an island of potential, the ground beneath him only a single dent on an ocean of thought and will, less complicated than the island of the Rada atop it who roamed far and wide, ever bringing more of what he saw and experienced into him. The enormity of it, one lone man and his choices and how they affected the whole of the vast ocean of thought and intent which made up the world, seeing it all at once overwhelmed Jad, like he was trying to understand the idea of a rainstorm from ripples on the surface of a lake.

Reluctantly, Jad looked up in awe, having a growing sense that if he had more time, if he were able to understand what he was seeing, there was much he could learn about the man—*the truth*—his choices, how he veered from one story to the next—*to here. And tomorrow…*

Tez, too … he recognized the same intricacy fountaining from him, except the motion of a broadening story slimmed to a point and faded, the rainstorm trickling to a drop … then evaporating. *Tez isn't here.* The soldier had ended him. Tez, too, had skimmed over the skin of the world, forging a new name for himself with each heavy step, each clipped breath, every angry word. And this myriad of Tez had severed here today with the poke of the Rada's knife. Like so much else today, Tez was ending, and he hated both Tez and the Rada for it. It was like unfalling the rain, unhearing a name…

If I hadn't insisted we bring the Rada back, Tez would still be alive.

The Rada's story was ending soon too, ripples of him merging to a single weak point, the potential boiling away.

Did he care? *Why should I help him? He killed Tez.*

In the distance, voices raised in anger again, many of them all shouting at once. Jad heard his father's voice as plainly as if he were sitting in the room with him.

It was then that he saw the ripples in the Rada's story change, strengthen. The weak rainstorm grew strong. The man's story would continue. That was clear.

The soldier can help Father. I have to try again.

Jad's mind bubbled like a simmering pot, his frustration heating as he turned his thoughts to doing whatever *trick* the Rada asked of him—he had to do it, there was no other way. His village, *Father, Mother, Miu*, everyone, needed him.

How far the ripples of the Rada spread, and how he had dappled his story into the world as he lived, changing the true name of himself and what he touched, was impossible to hold all at once—

But for one brief moment, Jad pulled back, taking it all in, drew himself up like a breath…

…raised his fists clasped over his head the way he would when wielding his crook, and as he flung his fists down hard onto the man's chest, hitting him with a thump, he saw it wasn't truly just his hands he was flinging low in frustration, it was his own complicated essence, his own burgeoning ripples of the places, the people, the potential of him had reached, even if it hadn't yet spread very far from his village—across the plain to Ren, out into the grasslands where the horse lords lived, a little wisp up into the white tips of the mountains and down the other side…

…yet with it Jad also felt a tenuous, searing sense of a vaster inhale being held just over his shoulder…

All this, like his fists he slammed down, colliding with the rainstorm of the Rada, hating that he was hanging all his hopes on the man.

And with his plea: *Fix him to help us kill the Phentinites!*

Jad fell back, numbness traveling through him.

He was mountains.

He was the plains stretching out to the horizon.

He was the great lake that opened to the south where the big trading boats came from.

The room trembled. Or was that the world?

He blinked and it was only the ceiling he saw, and in his ears that he heard the rumbling. He was Jad, the boy, here in this small, high village, pushing himself to his knees, hearing men yelling in the distance. Their voices washed into the room, collected in the corners, and flowed out over the floor, where they filtered away.

Father?

The Rada, coughing, flipping over onto his side, half on top of Tez, brought him back.

Did I smack him too hard? Curling into a ball, the soldier hacked a gooey line of red drool out behind his bedroll.

Jad stood, stepping back, not seeing potential shimmering from the man anymore, just the skinny, stinking stranger slipping in Tez's blood, smearing it over the cake of his own old filth so that the red made a sheen atop the crusted black. Rising to his hands and knees, the Rada spat a gross thick gob onto the floor near Tez's feet, and levered himself upright like a fighter who had been felled by a lucky punch. Slowly, he rose up a good head taller than Jad. The black circles under his eyes had faded. His skin looked browner than Jad's, if currently pale. Flexing his skinny arms and fingers, sly eyes rose to Jad's with a smile, holding the knife he had used to stab Tez in his dripping red hand, which with how stick-thin he was, looked like a gnarled, pointy branch.

"You did it," said the soldier with quiet surprise, looking healthy, happy. "By Ardo's overbite, you did it! Good boy … good … Jad," he said, jumping in place as if testing his legs. "I'm … alive. I feel *good*."

The soldier exploded toward Jad.

Jad lurched back. His was not a face Jad would trust, not this whole person. But the Rada's arms flung around him, hugged him close, tousling his hair, and the man spoke with a strong voice for the first time, deeper than Jad expected. "You did it, boy! You're one of them! Oh, we'll do great things together."

Where is his knife?

The man's chest, thin and hollow like a bird's, was a crust that stank like the village's killing stone. Yesterday's heat had long since soured all the old diseased blood over his chest.

The soldier released him. Jad peeled away to see the Rada's head cocked, listening. Distantly, shields were bashing a steady beat, like drums. The Rada sniffed the air. His demeanor had changed, his elation faded to a wary animal alertness.

"Phentinite pigs," he said. He bent and wiped his knife on Tez's sleeve, retrieving the spear. For good measure, Jad picked up his crook. When he looked up, the Rada was watching him with a fox's sidelong curiosity. "Thank you, boy," he said. "I told you I'd help. Now let me show you. You'll see. I'll show you right now. Let's go."

"Quiet through here, boy," said the Rada, crouching low, releasing branches swinging back his way. He had grabbed him by the collar when he'd tried to hurry down the middle of the path, yanking him into the trees, where Jad chose each step carefully, making little noise, even as the Rada came bent like a crow, hopping, twigs snapping beneath his feet. "They might have sent men circling around. Phin and his boys probably."

They had been hearing voices, loud and gruff, buzzing through the trees.

The closer they came, the heavier Jad felt, a stupid, childlike hesitation for disobeying. He wasn't supposed to be there.

Down by the river, the Rada pushed him out of the trees behind Zua's house, and they looked up the hill at the village, which had changed.

From the river, the land rose in a protected plain, upon which most of the village had been built, before sloping up gradually toward the foothills. A narrow, flat gap lay where families grew a few chickpeas and other plants, and it was along the edge of this even ground that the finished ditch, about as deep as Jad was tall, now encompassed about half the village. Long spikes stuck from the berm that had been raised above it, and atop the berm a fence had been erected—the kind of fence the village was good at, usually to corral sheep inside. The men of the village were arrayed behind it, facing soldiers clustered a hundred paces distant on the slope above.

Jad's terrible daydream came alive before him.

Stabbing, stabbing, into a killing pen.

Four orderly rows of soldiers stood as straight as a basket's binding. Their insectile rigidity, poised like a nest of hornets waiting outside a beehive, was made stranger, deadlier, as they all wore the same leather armor the Rada had been wearing when they'd found him in the river: leather greaves on their legs and arms; the blue feathers on their leather helmets matched the blue handprints splashed across their shields and the blue streaks down the sides of their faces. Round wicker shields held aloft, spears planted in the dirt, they could have been the same man repeated eighty times, all of them watchful, predatory.

Sandals, Jad noticed. They had definitely come from a warmer place.

It was a nonsense thought, something ordinary that lasted only a moment.

Near the armored soldiers, higher on the slope, stood twenty men in loose order, all of them with pouches and long straps slung over their shoulders. *Slingers.* Jad heard the word in Tez's voice. He liked to say it almost like a swear, as if not getting close enough to an enemy to be stabbed were cowardly. As if Tez had ever seen a real enemy.

Between the lines of soldiers and the village stood three men, two soldiers and a man with a beard. The nearest of the soldiers wore the same armor and plumes as the soldiers on the hillside, except the feather atop the helmet he had tucked under an arm was red, and red streaks splashed down his face and chest.

Behind him, the bearded man, wearing a green shirt and tall tailored hat, looked to be their guide. He should have guessed he would be one of the fat, fancy merchants from Ren who parted people in the streets like a boulder rolling through bullrushes.

It was the third man who caught Jad's attention. There had been talk of Phentinite encroachment on Ren for a couple years, but until today he had never laid eyes on real soldiers, and he had never guessed they could be adorned in such splendor. A slender, older man, chin held high, his shining silvery breastplate, and the metal greaves on his wrists and shins, captured the morning's amber sunlight. His helmet, also gleaming, raised to a blunt, fish-like point in the front, and fanned out in the back like a broad, angular tail. It took a moment for Jad to realize the patterns across the front of his forehead were supposed to be sharp teeth. The smooth red sash draped over one of his shoulders rippled as he leaned toward their guide, and then spoke to the soldier in front of him, who nodded.

The merchant next to him sounded as pompous as he looked: "The Phentinite masters are content to overlook the rudeness of our greeting here today," he called down the hillside. "They would like to remind you that the great god eater, Shangar, now resides in Ren with two hundred more soldiers. You need not throw away your lives like this."

There was grumbling from behind the berm, the men looking at one another.

It all seemed unreal. Even now Jad could close his eyes and if someone told him the past few days had been a dream, a terrible, anxious nightmare, and he could wake up, he could believe it. Even the sunny calm of the morning could be fed to him happily. How many times had he sleepily come stretching into the village to see the long shadows from the treetops slashing toward the river the way they were this morning? Normally it foretold a pleasant day ahead, easy wrangling of the ewes, or sitting with his feet cooling in the shallows of the river, cornering little fish. It was how normal the morning seemed otherwise, when he knew it couldn't be, and wouldn't ever be again, that made the breath catch in his throat.

"Gardin," the Rada muttered next to Jad, as if to himself, "you cocky shit. Look at him preening up there with his fancy red feather. That shiny Phentinite pig got his hand up his ass."

Jad's attention went to the soldier in front wearing the leather armor with the red feather. With his broad face and squinting, calculating eyes, he looked like any man in the village, capable and sure—half twisting to hear the shining man behind him while never fully turning his attention from the line of Jad's people behind the berm in the village.

The Rada kept glaring at the man while Jad looked for his father, and spotted him on the line, Tez's father and Methen nearby, watching the armored foreigners have their discussion. With all eyes on the soldiers, he and the Rada hadn't been seen yet.

"That's all of them, boy," said the Rada animatedly. "No one sneaking around. I'll fix this. You follow me until we get up there by the house. Then you scarper on over inside the fence to your own kind, you got that?" Jad nodded, feeling hollow now that the time had come to be seen. "You go up there, they're liable to grab you, gut you, maybe throw you to those no-chin slingers for some fun. I go in there with you, your people probably going to hook my guts out. But you just watch. I said I would help, didn't I? Didn't I?"

Jad nodded.

"Good. This is it, boy. I'm going to make this all better. You watch me. Then when the time is right, you do whatever it is you have to do, okay? Your speaker words. You understand?"

Jad shook his head. What had happened back there in their house felt like a half-remembered dream. "What do I do?"

The Rada shrugged. "Your speaker words. Burn them all alive. Turn their wieners to worms. Cinch their armor so their eyes pop. Mush the ground under their feet into dung so they sink in past their ears. Your choice."

Jad nodded anyway.

"Smart boy." The Rada's hand on Jad's back pushed him forward. "Don't fill your pants when the time comes. Last enemy speaker we Rada caught, we cut his tongue and eyes out and lashed him between two of the moving stones of Sonbry."

The Rada's surprisingly strong hand pushed him out from the trees. Jad felt like a rabbit breaking cover, wary of owls. Only a few minutes had passed since he'd seen Tez stabbed in the face, his sliced cheek hanging open like fish skin.

That was what a person was, meat and blood. Jad was extra aware of his body as he ran.

They were only a few paces out before Jad angled for the fence. "We'll show those shits," he heard the Rada mutter behind him. "Pig sons of whores."

Tumbling down into the trench in his hurry to get to safety, Jad slipped in his scramble to get up the other side, which were dark, slick, mucky, and he tried levering himself up with his crook. His back felt exposed as mud smeared over Tez's blood that had dried black on his knees.

Darson's face was looking down at him from the fence when he reached up for a handhold. "Come to bite some Phentinite ankles, Jad?" the man laughed. "Get up here." Darson's hand fell on him, steadying him. "Some of these blue fuckers is pretty tall. Stab straight out, boy. Catch 'em in the dick."

He was still laughing as he helped Jad over the stakes and through the fence, as if it really were an ordinary morning and they were down catching fish in the river and he had just plopped a worm in Aunt Beatti's tea when she wasn't looking.

Doubt dropped through Jad when he saw the shock on his father's face. "Jad?" he heard him say, dismay in his tone. Everyone turned his way.

Now they all knew he wasn't helping with the flocks.

Their attention left him when the Rada started yelling, coming out from behind one of the houses: "Gardin, you traitorous shit, why are you letting yourself be l—?"

"Orda!" blurted the soldier with the red feather and slashes, turning from conferring with the shining soldier behind him. There was a lot to hear in that one word, both surprise and contempt, as plain as the wind.

It occurred to Jad that until now he hadn't known the Rada's name. *Orda*.

The Rada strutted up to within three strides of the three men, what seemed a brash closeness, practically striking distance. The merchant retreated two paces. The two men in armor were empty-handed, but long leather sheaths hung at their sides. They had *swords*. Jad had heard of them from Tez. They were like long, heavy knives.

Tez.

Meat and blood.

Tate left his part of the line along the berm to clomp over to Father. "How in all of Zua's creation is that rotten boneshit walking? Was he faking it all this time?"

Father shrugged, agitated. "I don't know, Tate."

That answer wasn't good enough for Tez's father. The big man's eyes found Jad's, and Jad tried not to think of Tez in a pool of smeared blood back in his house—Tez's blood soaked over his knees. But Tate stared down at him, and then looked up into the distance with an expression of unease unlike Jad had ever seen him wear.

He knows. Jad was sure of it.

Father looked like he had more to say too, but there was no time. The Rada had squared himself up before the two armored soldiers. Unlike his half voice when lying injured on the floor, the man spoke loudly, brash.

"Nice morning to kill more good people for the Phentinite pigs, eh, Gardin?"

The slender soldier in the shiny fish armor leaned toward the commander with the red feather—to Gardin. Jad was close enough now to hear: "*Te blen seh Orda nos pincas brenandier ta me sous malis?*" The man made no attempt to keep quiet, so his rich, clear voice floated easily to the village thirty paces down the hillside.

Jad noticed the merchant smile to himself. The red-feathered commander replied to the soldier in shining armor with a nod, then assessed the Rada up and down. Where the first man had a voice for commanding servants, this one had a plain, straightforward tone, a voice for commanding men:

"*Blen seh te.* How did you get here, Orda?"

"Came out of my mother," said the Rada. "Hasn't anyone ever told you how it works, Gardin?"

"*Men ta dit* nendos *dender seh pendum,*" sneered the man in the shiny armor, seeming to ignore the Rada.

It was easy to see the Rada nearly danced in place with agitation for being dismissed. Jad could understand him and the commander, *Gardin*, just fine, but wished he knew what the soldier in the shiny armor was saying. He seemed to be in charge.

As soon as he thought it, Jad felt the air still around him, the Zuan men around him quieting, just briefly.

"*Ta sa* flea, not me!" blurted the Rada, pointing at the commander in the shiny armor. "A flea sucking the blood from the Radene people and a dozen other cities. It's time you were pinched off!"

The red-feathered commander threw his hand up, cutting the Rada off. The soldier in the shiny armor had drawn himself taller, seemingly ignoring the Rada yelling at him, and this time when he spoke, Jad understood him perfectly:

"Yes, Gardin ... it seems your report that *scouts* killed your traitor as he tried to desert were not entirely reliable..."

"Sure," said the Rada quickly, as if telling a joke, to the apparent dismay of the red-feathered soldier. "It was scouts. They were scouting all over for me outside Gardin's tent. Bonesy's good with dice, and Pep can piss farther than anyone with his thin whistle dick, but weak as kittens, both of them. Gave me a few scratches, but I came—"

"It was a Rada problem," interrupted the commander loudly, turning fully to the slender man. "We Rada took care of it."

"Don't interrupt me anymore, Gardin!" the Rada yelled, losing his composure. "I will be heard! All of the Rada will hear me!" He gestured largely to the soldiers arrayed in rows up on the hill, who had stood like statues all this time. "The Rada won't be slaves to these Phentinite pigs anymore!"

"He has one thing correct," said the slender man, "the Rada are a nuisance, much like any pest. Perhaps Radene's lesson has not been adequately learned…?"

All along the berm, the men of the village were looking to one another, not sure what they should make of the exchange.

"Forgive me, Overseer," said the commander. "I don't know how this could have happened. This man is a criminal and a traitor to the empire, to all of Rada, and to Shangar. He is … a fool. Like you said, a flea." He removed his sword from its leather. It was bronze and glinted in the morning light. All along the berm, the men of the village craned forward, following its shine as the commander bowed before the overseer, going to one knee with his brilliant sword's tip sharp into the soft, grassy loam of the hillside. "Even among our own people, but especially beneath the notice of your eminence."

The Rada threw his hands up dramatically and laughed, even turning behind him to look at Jad and the line of their village, as if to share the joke. "Gardin, you idiot! Don't bow to this fattened Phentinite pig. Get off your knees. This is the time, don't you see? Look at me standing here whole before you. Remember my limp? Remember how I squinted? Look at me now. I can see just fine. And watch…" The Rada did a short, almost drunken dance in place, jocular and scornful. "I was just foolin'. Bonesy got in a good whack across my leg, here. Pep run me right through with that spear of his. But look at me now, good as new. *Commander*, now is the time to command *our* people in the true fight against these pigs—just like you planned, just like we dreamed of. Ardo brought us to this place for a reason. He's young, but these people have a young sp—"

The Rada didn't have a chance to finish. The commander rose from kneeling to the overseer, his sword flashing in the crisp autumn sun as it came cleaving down into the Rada's neck.

Jad and all the men behind the berm flinched as one.

The bronze sword hacked deep into the Rada in a way a spear or an arrow never could, cutting a deep, fibrous wound. Stumbling back, the Rada screamed a bray they all recognized, a creature's death wail, which were all alike despite the creature, man or animal—guttural and wild—and another ripple went through the Zuans behind the fence. An awful bray like that burrowed down into a body in a way one couldn't guard against. It spoke directly to the soul.

The sword stuck from the Rada's neck like a stick rammed through a fish's gills to carry it home. The blow had driven him to his knees, and Jad couldn't see, but he looked to be gaping up into the face of his former commander, his arms spread like limp wings, surprisingly still holding what used to be Tez's spear in one outstretched hand. The birds had long since quit their morning songs, and on both sides men made no movement, the Rada's fractured death gurgle the only noise on the hillside.

"Zua's dick..." muttered Darson next to Jad.

Metal scraped bone as the commander put his foot up onto the Rada's shoulder and pulled the sword free, practically from the top of his ribs.

The Rada's spear tipped from his hand into the grass.

"How's he still alive?" someone nearby muttered.

"Shut up and die already!" yelled one of the soldiers from up on the hill, one of the slingers, to some laughter.

But the Rada's bray to the sky, gruff and mournful, was not weakening.

"S'right," said Darson. "Shut up sooner the better," trying to laugh and failing, shaking his head as if the Rada's wail were lodged in his ears like water.

Finally, the Rada slumped, a long wet, slurp of air still sucking through him as the commander turned, flicking blood from the weapon and moving it to his other hand.

"Effective," said the overseer with a shudder, "if garish, Gardin. Now, what was it he was saying about the true—?"

Not for a moment did the overseer expect to be punched in the face. His expression stayed the same superior, bored sneer right up until Gardin's fist crunched against his nose. Blood splattered down across his shiny armor.

Metal knuckles, Jad remembered, men all along the line bristling next to him, looking on as the overseer stumbled back, mouth open, eyes comically wide. He slid on the grass and thudded to the ground like a wobbly, newborn ewe. The goose honk he made as he sucked for air was not as dignified as his armor, the helmet of which rolled clinking down the hill—or as loud as the Rada's death moan, who had finally collapsed into a heap nearby, muffled if not yet silent—amazingly still alive.

They watched as the commander made little fanfare of approaching the overseer, drawing his sword back.

"Wait, no!" the overseer yelled nasally, coughing on blood.

The commander didn't hesitate. He had an efficiency about him, how he stood, how he spoke, and spent no extra effort in plunging his already purpled sword into the man's neck above his metal collar. It looked like an act of resignation, the last nail to hammer, the final shovelful of dirt—a job to be done. This was more like the killing of an animal they all recognized, determined and silent.

The overseer's body stiffened, kicking his silvery legs into the muddied hillside, but unlike the Rada—who was still holding himself up on his knees—the shining armor immediately plopped to the side, limp, lifeless.

Jad nearly missed the final stroke. As soon as the punch landed, on the hill a number of Rada soldiers broke formation, not charging down the hill like he'd first feared, but to his surprise dashing towards the lines of slingers. Spears flashed, and many of the lightly armored slingers fell screaming, protesting, as sharp bronze poised up and plunged down.

Father grabbed Jad by the collar and pulled him lower behind the barricade, exchanging uncertain glances with the other men, not sure what to make of what was happening.

Not Darson, next to Jad, who stayed standing. "One less, two less, that's three…" he muttered.

Jad couldn't understand what the slingers were yelling. Just gibberish. Panicking in all directions, many of them ran for the forest with the blue-feathered Rada soldiers leaping deftly into the brush after them, shouting directions, coordinating—some of them cheering and laughing.

The commotion faded. The heavier the silence, the heavier Jad felt the weight inside of him. Out on the middle of the hillside, the commander had not moved during the chaos, gazing up into the sky as if exhausted.

Jad could *still* hear the Rada's—*Orda's*—resilient death groan even from thirty paces. Tears welled up and Jad pinched them from his eyelashes before they could fall. What had been the point of him fixing the man? He hadn't helped. He hadn't even tried to dodge the sword through his neck. Sheep were smarter than that.

The commander turned back toward where the Rada was still kneeling, bent over as if in patient prayer.

Jad could hear the breath of every man in line with him, the blood pounding in his ears, the distant cry of a hawk miles out over the plains.

"Orda, you idiot, too stubborn even to die," said the red-feathered Rada commander, rubbing at a large triangle of the overseer's black blood across his cheek. "Do you know what you've done? These people could have been part of the empire, far from Eriim. Five years from now, the prancing Phentinite princes will forget about their alliance with the horse lords and wander off to stick their pointy noses someplace else they don't belong. Now ... thanks to you ... all these people—what are they, farmers? fishermen?—now they have to die so they never tell anyone what they've heard here."

Jad clenched his fists. He looked down the line, but none of the other men, braver than him, had moved, and he fought his instinct to run.

A scream rose over the trees and cut off sharply—one of the slingers. The sharpened sticks and sheep fence in front of the village seemed suddenly less likely to stop these orderly lines of armored killers.

Jad swallowed hard. Time was short. *What was it the Rada wanted me to do?*

As the commander turned to the fifty or so soldiers remaining on the hill, raising his fist, the Rada stirred, pushing himself up onto his hands and knees.

"By Zua's..." Darson said, trailing off.

As their commander raised his fist, the soldiers hefted their shields as one to form a wall, and began tromping down the hill toward the village, almost resignedly.

"Impossible," Jad heard someone say.

The Rada wasn't dead. The man's head rose from his chest.

"Gardin," they heard him growl, gruffly, like he was gargling the words. "You shit."

The Rada pushed himself back to his knees.

The commander retreated a step in disbelief. Then the Rada got one foot beneath him. Then pushed himself to his feet, swaying. His filthy undershirt, having been cleaved, fell down over his arm. His shoulder, which a few moments ago had been halved by the sword, had since knitted together. A pink seam remained of where the meat had separated, and as they watched that pink seam blackened again, his bloody, bruised flesh pressing itself together.

On the hill, many of the marching soldiers halted, stumbling out of cohesion.

The Rada spat a long gob of thick, gooey, blood into the dirt by his feet. "For these pigs?" asked the Rada, wiping his mouth. "I bring you ... these people ... that boy ... could be Radene's savior!"

The commander's stunned expression never changed as the Rada yelled at him, and just like when he punched the overseer in the nose, he gave no indication that he was about to attack before he plunged forward and drove his bloodied sword through the man again.

The Rada cried out, stumbling into him, but this was no death wail, no story but pain. He bowed low but kept his feet.

"For these pigs!" Jad heard him grunt, with derision and disappointment, pulling back from his former commander's violent embrace, looking up at him hatefully. Slowly, like a black cloud's inexorable approach after gathering above a high peak, he reached up and grasped him by the shoulder.

A look of horror had frozen on Gardin's face. Trying to tug his sword back that was sticking out of the Rada's back, he was too close; he couldn't.

Taking him by the wrist, the Rada stopped him. "That hurts," he said. And suddenly he had a knife in his other hand.

The commander protested, his stalwart tone lost to panic. "It wasn't the time, Orda! The overseer, he—"

The Rada slashed. The commander let go of his sword's hilt and stumbled back, a deep gash across the underside of his arm. And when the man tripped over the dead overseer's leg on the ground, the Rada followed, jumped down on top of him, pressing him back into the green, sheep-shorn grass, slashing the knife down into his neck, fighting to push his weight higher up onto the man's chest for leverage, slicing his hands and arms out of the way, *click-click metal on bone*, surging up and slamming the knife sliding down again and again off the man's cheeks and chin, his neck, his collar. The Rada stood his whole body behind the knife.

"For these pigs?" The blade bit down into the man's neck.

"For these pigs!" The blade squelched down into his eye.

"These pigs!" The Rada kept stabbing until the knife had long been coming down undefended and he slowed, spent.

A few breaths. It was over.

The Rada sat back, the wet huff of his hard breathing blowing up as autumn vapor. He cleared his throat, spit to the side, still red, thick, gross. Only then did he seem to notice the sword dangling out of him. He grasped its hilt, and inch by inch withdrew it from his chest. Echoes of his grunts bounced off the walls of Zua's house.

"What is he?" muttered Darson.

Both hillside and village, the soldiers and the shepherds, watched him pulling the sword until the tip fell out. Then he lurched back, getting his feet beneath him, wobbled to his full height, sword tip dangling limp down into the dirt. He wiped his brow, and it looked like he drew his palm across the sword's edge deliberately, to see how sharp it was, before looking behind him toward the village, his thin chest heaving. He gave a short wave.

Jad heard the men murmur, but did not look round.

The Rada then faced his own people on the hill. They had stopped advancing when Gardin had fallen. It had happened so quickly. Slack now, like supple spring grass, they stared on, the Rada looking back, and it took a few moments before the first one of them sank to one knee. A moment later, most of them had, some resting to both. With care, they removed their helmets and set them in the stubby grass before them. One hand on the leather of their helms, they held a fist over their hearts, and bowed their heads.

The Rada kicked the commander's limp foot in the grass. "Yeah, I suppose he wasn't all bad," he yelled up at them. His voice wasn't the same. *From being hacked nearly in two.* It came deeper, more guttural.

After a moment of regarding the soldiers, with a sigh he knelt as well. He had no helmet to take off, but pressed his fist to his heart.

Next to Jad, Darson made another disbelieving noise. "Whoever's dreaming this, dig us up some pretty girls."

I'm having this dream, Jad thought, a strange, lightheaded, churning elation rushing through him, and not for the sight of so much blood. *I did this.*

Tez's father was glaring at him, and Jad only realized he was smiling after he felt it slide from his face.

Last of the soldiers to kneel, the Rada was the first to stand, a metallic ting as he scraped the commander's bloodied sword up from the dirt to lean on it. He clapped grass from his knees.

"Well … there was a time when he was a fine man," he called up the hill to the soldiers. "But we have to stay strong. Now … I mean to have his armor for my own. Not this Phentinite pig armor, but the rest. These greaves. These guards. Nicely made. Good Radene leather. So … I know what some of you want, and I don't blame you. Come avenge your fallen commander if you can."

"Stray cur," growled one of the soldiers.

"You won't win," replied the Rada. "Attack me and you die. I'm not the man I was."

"You would have to be a man first!" another soldier yelled down.

What is he doing? thought Jad. For a moment he had dared hope it was all over. The Rada had killed their leaders. *Is it done? Will they go home?*

The Rada had helped, like he had promised. But now he seemed to be inviting them to attack.

Masom had been right in assessing the attackers' numbers. Eighty or ninety men, with a contingent of slingers. Stragglers returning out of the trees with blood-spattered greaves from hunting the slingers joined the fifty or so men arrayed before them now, looking to one another questioningly. Much had changed in the few minutes they had been gone.

"We don't need to fight each other," said the Rada. "Together, we can take Radene back from the Phentinite pigs. Follow me, and the Darine River will flow with invader pigs' blood."

Would they listen? Would they leave?

Many of the soldiers were rising to their feet, knocking their helmets down atop their heads firmly. They loosened their shoulders and kicked their feet into the dirt for firmer grip, like a ram readying to charge.

No one answered.

The Rada raised his commander's bronze sword. It no longer caught the light. "Radene's might has been held down too long."

The first soldiers started drumming their shields with their spears as more of them stood, donned their helmets, and joined in the chorus of drumming, growing louder, until all the men arrayed across their lines were now standing, now all in sync, now their thumping booming like thunder.

The Rada lowered the sword. "Fine," he spat, when he could be heard. "Come get me, then."

In response, the soldiers hefted their shields high, spears piercing the air between them.

"For Rada!" one yelled.

"For Gardin!" another answered. Many others took up the call.

A great roar shivered the hillside. Jad felt the ground rumble.

The air shook as all fifty of the soldiers pushed off, charging down the slope toward the Rada, toward the village, their earlier lockstep, their order forgotten, each man urging forward as if vying to be first. Jad was reminded again of the lightning striking the trees, the power rushing through the pasture below the sheer cliffs.

He went rigid with fear, unable to look away from the scrawny, shirtless Rada standing his ground in the path of the charging soldiers, yelling the same cry back at them. The man raised his stolen sword and swung it back and forth like a club as the men bore down on him.

Jad wondered if he knew how to use that sword.

It took only moments. Jad had time to see two spear tips burst from the Rada's back. The skinny Rada, armorless, didn't fall. He grabbed one of the spears, holding it fast inside his body the same way he had held the commander's sword a few minutes ago, swinging that same sword up now to catch the unsuspecting soldier in the thigh. The last Jad saw, the Rada was turning to the other spear's owner, who was trying to wrench it back out of the Rada's chest, then the other sixty screaming soldiers came leaping across the trench around the village into the midst of their defensive spikes, lunging with their long spears. A fist-size stone sailed over the berm and crunched into Tate's left shoulder.

Jad was hauled back from the top of the berm. "Straight in the dick, boy!" yelled Darson as he pushed Jad behind him. "Straight in the dick!"

"Zua will protect us!" yelled Methen down the line reassuringly, lunging forward with his sharpened stick.

The soldiers' sharp bronze tips came leaping up the berm. The fire-blackened spears of the village thrust back to meet them. The determined roar that rose from the men of the village proved equal to that of the soldiers fighting to cross the stakes.

"Push them back!" yelled Tate as they all leapt to the line, spears outthrust, meeting the Phentinites' armor and grim faces with the thud of meat slapping together. Already the sides were stuck together between the stakes like intertwined thistles. Men screamed and bodies fell.

Jad spied his father by his beard and broad shoulders, dodging a spear's thrust and stabbing down into the trench, only to take a nick in the shoulder from another soldier.

Limp bodies tangled on the stakes and slid down the berm. It was no good. The Phentinites had broad shields to hide behind and stab from, and outnumbered them two to one. His father and the men had only what boards they'd lashed together during the night.

And the soldiers had fought before.

Stones came flying over the berm from all directions, unexpected and deadly, the thud they made when they smacked a meaty shoulder like beating a carpet with a broom. The men of the village had no helmets, and Father's cousin took his eyes off the man in front of him to look at the man behind him aiming a stone only to take a spear through the throat.

Jad inched back from the death and the stink of blood and shit. *Phentinites stabbing, stabbing, into a killing pen.*

Jad saw Methen crumple back holding his thigh, blood spewing from it.

What am I supposed to do?

He remembered the Rada saying: *Turn their little snakes into wiggly worms ... call fire from the sky ... turn their weapons to smoke...*

Movement between the houses. Soldiers were sneaking around to come at them from the side.

Jad jumped back as with a loud *whump* big Darson toppled like a felled tree back from the top of the berm, folding in a heap at his feet. His face and forehead were smashed in like an egg, his eye squeezed out and peering up past Jad at an impossible direction.

Tall and streaked with blue paint down his face, a soldier filled the gap in the line Darson had left. Up close, his chest armor appeared pitted from past blows. Scars marred the man's cheek to his chin, and blood painted his arms. He looked down at Jad with a quick smile more dangerous-seeming than the jagged metal knuckles protruding from his hand holding his spear.

Jad, on his back, to protect himself raised his father's crook.

Then the spiked soldier's tongue popped out of his mouth and a spear followed up through his throat. The soldier had enough time to look surprised before his shoulders went limp. Then the Rada, half the man's size, the hair down his chest mottled with clumps of purply gore, pulled his spear back and watched as the man slid on his face down the berm to lie unmoving next to Darson.

"If I'm not a man, what's that make you, Plon?" he sneered.

In between his ribs, as if separating them, three spears jutted from his body.

The spears have to hit bones, Jad thought mindlessly. *He's so skinny.*

Jad raised his crook higher, amazed, horrified. How was he still alive?

The Rada had come up behind the soldiers unexpectedly. Their leather armor little protected them along the sides and back of the neck, and before the nearest soldier could react, the Rada turned and jammed the metal tip of his spear up into the man's exposed armpit. With a silent gasp, the soldier crumpled and fell, rolling back down the ditch, and three of his nearby companions pivoted in surprise, scanning to see if any more attackers had snuck up behind.

The Rada cast a hurried glance at Jad over his shoulder. "End this, boy!"

One of the soldiers didn't hesitate to exploit the opening. Lunging forward, he ran the shirtless Rada through. Blood spattered the soldier's chest and face. The Rada, *Orda*, bore the brunt of the blow, staggering back, but kept his feet, looking annoyed.

"Bonesy, you pimpled anus…"

He grasped the spear by the haft and drew back, pulling the larger soldier with him, his knife in his hand again slashing out like some tenacious river creature gnashing at a hungry bear, ripping a deep gash across the man's arms. The soldier relinquished his spear, blood dripping from his wrist, and all three soldiers fell back, waving their weapons uncertainly.

"What happened to you, Orda?" the bleeding soldier asked breathlessly.

The Rada's spear having cracked, he threw it aside, and with a grimace grasped one of the three shafts sticking out from beneath his ribs.

"I have become Arda's wrath…" he said, teeth gritted, the soldiers watching in horror as he drew the spear out, screaming all the while, and then squared up and stalked fearlessly toward them. "I will be Radene's revenge."

Two soldiers stumbled back and ran. The third slipped and slid into the ditch and out of sight.

"What happened to *you*, Bonesy? Come back!" he yelled after the retreating men. Anger folded through the Rada's limbs, and with a grunt he speared an unsuspecting soldier behind the fleeing men and the man fell with his helmet askew.

"Do it, boy!" the Rada yelled over his shoulder. "Put the fear into them!"

I should be helping, Jad thought. He had hunkered down when Darson fell. *I need to be helping.* His legs wouldn't work until he told them to, but slowly he trembled to his full height. *I need to be brave.*

He told his arms to raise the crook high.

Fire … speakers … call fire from the sky, the Rada had said.

Is that something I can do?

"Do it, boy!" yelled the Rada from somewhere down the berm with a shriek of pain. "Show them!"

The tip of his crook wavered near Darson's smashed face. He would bring it down the same way he had in the meadow. He would bring down … he would bring down … *fire*. Make the Phentinites pay for this blood, this death. *Radene's revenge. Zua's punishment…*

No … *Jad's* punishment. He gripped his crook tightly. *Fire…*

Jad saw the rock that hit him. It *thocked* high off one of the spikes, careened toward him, growing larger—there was a crack of light and the ground pitched sideways. The last thing Jad saw was Darson's blank, skewed expression, like he was still thinking of a joke even in death, staring at him from a foot away.

He heard a rush as if he were underwater. Then, feeling serene, everything turned blurry.

Jad awoke, a tickle on his face. He had been hearing the wind in the trees for a while.

He brushed at the tickle, brought a sharp sticky pin close to his nose to look at it. A little sword of a pine needle.

Evening had come, yet the dim light still hurt his eyes, strange shadows dancing in from somewhere outside the house.

House?

Wind was blowing over his face. Only now did he realize the movement he had been seeing above him came from swaying branches. He'd been half dreaming that they were muddy hands, pushing, pushing him into the earth. He couldn't move. They rose as high as the sky.

He was beneath his broad pine tree, where he had slept last night.

His face felt sticky. He touched rough fabric around his head. A bandage.

As he awoke, so did the growing awareness that some of what he thought was the rumbling of the wind was actually throbbing in his head. His lips were rough, parched for water.

Raising himself up and crawling out from beneath the branches made his head hurt worse than he'd ever felt before— even the wind hurt on his cheeks—but he had to find his father. He had to see if he was still alive.

His shortened shadow walked sidelong. He expected to see

yellow holes in it where his eyes would be. When he squeezed them shut it felt like the light shone right through him, searing his mind, unsettling his stomach. The sharp yellow leaves flashed above, and from somewhere he heard shouts, the ringing clunk of striking stone. *Spears or shovels?* He kept his head down and followed the sound down toward Zua's shrine.

As he came around the last house, peering down at the fenced-in village below but only able to steal glimpses before his eyes hurt too much, he wasn't sure what he was seeing.

A lot of men were lying on the ground, most around the ditch; a few were walking among them near the line of their stakes and fences, and though in some cases they had donned the helmets and armor of the Phentinites, they were men he recognized, the men of their village.

At the edge of the village, stripped of their armor, a pile of naked bodies were stacked three high, white-bellied in the bright autumn sun like dead fish. *Phentinites.* The dead of the village lay in a neat row before Zua's shrine.

Is Father—?

"Jad," he heard his name being called, softly, hurriedly. "Jad, come…"

At a limping run, his father came cantering down the hill from out of the trees and took him by the shoulder, as if shielding him from view of the village. He hugged Jad close. Jad didn't want to let go. His head hurt too much to bear it on his own.

"It's not a good idea to be here right now, son. How about me and you go fetch your mother and Miu. I think they'll be happy to see us."

Jad wanted to sit and close his eyes, but his father, arm around him, urged him along.

He nodded.

They had won, Father told him, as Jad made his third passage that day along the trail toward the cliffside pasturage.

Jad took short steps. Every one hurt his head. And when, after a thousand paces or so, he began flagging, falling even farther behind, Father scooped him up without a word and carried him.

"I told him you were dead," his father said. "After all the ... when the killing stopped, the Rada came looking for you ... after the soldiers turned and ran ... I tell you, it was something else—he was tearing into them like a fox into a rabbit, those big fierce warriors. About twenty of them were dead just all by himself. They stopped fighting us and turned toward him. Else they would have got a spear upside the head, one by one. Or maybe ... you ever see a squirrel try to protect its nuts from a bear cub? That's what it reminded me of. And they just ... a few of them stood around watching while they poked him full of holes, cut him half to ribbons, and still he kept on coming. Cuts kept healing. It was like trying to attack the rain or the sunshine, for all the good it did them.

"When it was done ... a lot of them gave up and left—a number of them had already taken their leader's body. That's when he came to me, him and a few other soldiers. He was covered in blood from the tip of his head to his bare toes. He asked me where you were. Said he was taking you with him. So ... I said you were dead. And Methen, he said so too. He saw you get hit square in the head with a stone and said you were killed. I guess he already saw you lying there on the ground...

"He had this look in his eye... I was ... I was glad to see him go. I was glad to see all of them go. Zua be praised."

An endless stream of Father's thoughts fell out of him. Jad strained to listen. But as they passed over the plain where he had fought Tez and then had called the birds and the flocks and...

"Let me down," said Jad. It didn't feel right to be carried like a baby here.

Father did, reluctant to do so, but happy to hear him talking again.

"How does it feel to be dead?" his father asked him as they trod along, slow again.

Jad's head was hurting worse, full of prickly light.

"It feels…"

He looked out over the shattered grass. Sun lay thickly between the bent stalks now. Too thickly. He wasn't sure what to say.

Miu ran to greet them. Mother clutched a handful of grass to bless Zua. Then she came too.

Jad slept in the shadow of the great cliffs. When he awoke feeling slightly better, the other flocks were gone. Only his family remained.

Mother wasn't nearly as happy when the next day Father prepared for he and Jad to take the flocks back to the autumn pasturage.

"Just until things settle," his father told her. "When all the knives are back in our belts."

Seven Zuan men had been killed in the battle. A great pyre bloodened the sky beneath the heavy clouds that evening. The bodies of the Phentinites had been thrown into the river, hopefully to drift downstream back to their masters. Whether that was smart or not didn't seem to matter.

The fences remained. The ditches filled with muddy rainwater.

Father scratched incessantly at the spear wound on his shoulder as they traversed the familiar path away from the village, herding the ewes ahead of them. Mother had scolded him to stop picking at it all morning, and to reapply the poultice of honey every evening, and to never neglect his devotions to Zua for renewed health.

Jad kept waiting for someone to ask him about Tez, even

just to speak his name. But no one did, at least where he could hear. Father had asked him to sleep under the pine again for just one more night, he thought as Tez's body still lay in their home, but when he had snuck down early, just after sunrise, there was no trace of him, not a smear of all the blood that had oozed across their floor.

Two days later, high in the windy plateau beneath snow-topped peaks, the snow lower now than it had been just the week before, Jad and his father finished fixing the gaps in the meadow's small shelter that the winter storms had pried open. Father did most of the work, as Jad's head still hurt, and he was coaxed to sleep as much as he wanted while there were still warm patches of afternoon sun.

Even with the shelter repaired and a thick blanket, he shivered that night, but at least if he were awake and sitting out amongst the ewes for warmth in the middle of the meadow, thinking about all that had happened, he wasn't laden with nightmares of clanking soldiers, plagued by a bone-deep weariness, sorrowful and lonely, that pushed him to wait for the dawn alone instead.

After the mist rose the next morning like drawing a white cloth away from a warm meal, he and Father stopped to watch a thin black line in the distance rising into the sky.

"That's Ren," his father said pensively.

"Smoke?" Jad asked.

"Something big burning."

That was all his father would say about that.

As the moon shrank to about half what it was, it was apparent the grass here was already feeling winter's withering, and the sheep could only nibble the stiff little knives for so long.

There was no lambing, no shearing to do, no cheese for them to make. Jad didn't want to talk and Father didn't push him, though he seemed restless.

The wind over the high mountain peaks had the most to say, usually late at night when it believed it was alone, but Jad heard it.

At no time did Jad ever feel that itch on the back of his neck like they were being watched. That made it easier to feel like they were the only people alive, peering down into the world from the rim. Everything that had happened to the village that day had the air of a dream. Only at night, when there was no other choice, when dreams rudely shook him awake, did it seem real.

Every now and then he would see Father standing on some high rock, staring out over the plains toward Ren. There had been no more smoke, and no word from the village. Normally, by now they would have made their autumn trek to the town to trade for winter goods. Father was probably itching to go before the first snows fell.

When the moon was nearly gone, Father told Jad to prepare to return. "Should be enough time," he said.

Enough time for what? Jad wondered.

They soon battened down their small repaired shelter for the winter, hoping it was sturdy enough again to resist the snowpress, and struck out for lower pastures.

In the day that it took to make their way home, Jad realized that while he missed his mother, missed Miu, he didn't miss the village. The village he saw when they came around the bed, stitched and scarred with trenches, and where bodies had bled into the ground, it wasn't the village he used to know.

Miu, at least, she was the same, and came running to greet both him and Father, and then hugged her favorites among the flock.

Mother smiled, happy to see them, if she stayed a little quiet. That evening, she urged Miu to go play with her friend Jillian at her place, then went out and came back with Methen.

"Don't say anything about Masom," Mother warned them in

a hushed voice. And that was how Jad learned that Masom had been dead these past weeks.

Even if Jad hadn't been told, he might have known it as soon as he saw Methen. Methen balanced his importance on his chin, but now rapped at their door quietly, announced himself with a voice that plunked to the floor by his feet, and sat in their home letting his pipe burn down with a dimmed light in his eyes.

With him, Methen had brought a winter's supply of salt and other seasonings, and new, proper boots, as Father had been braying all summer about how the holes in his toes kept getting larger.

"Made the trip to Ren already?" asked Father, almost sounding hurt.

"Ren came to us," Methen explained. "A caravan of five or six donkeys, three merchants. Pretty much anything we could ever want."

"Them fat, fancy fools," said Father, surprised, "all the way up here? What did they want?"

Methen gave him a little smile. "Haven't you heard, Jobus, there's good money to be made in selling metal. And when it's already been made into weapons…"

Father nodded.

"We didn't trade them all. We have a fair store of them now. Plus a little armor, and many leather strips." Methen slid a handful of clay markers across the floor to Father.

"What are these?" Father asked.

"Present these chits to any of the merchants by the dock in Ren," explained Methen. "The markings mean that you have already traded for goods … for a certain amount."

"How much?"

Methen swept his arm over the stuff he'd brought. "Enough for five years of salt and boots, at least. Zua has been good to us." He had flashes of the old Methen. He was always a good one to get better deals for you with the merchants in Ren. He and they seemed cut from the same cloth. But for the first time Jad wondered who would believe him now when he sold the blessings of Zua's protection.

Father sat back, stunned. He almost smiled, before he remembered where the good fortune had come from.

I wonder how Masom died, thought Jad. He wanted to ask. *Bravely*, for sure.

But for no reason, chided a small, ashamed part of himself.

"There's more," said Mother, when Father seemed about to thank Methen for the news, maybe clap him on the back and stand, footsore after a day's walking on a limping leg.

Methen nodded. "They came with word too, the merchants…"

"The Phentinites, they're all gone," said Mother. "Or dead."

"Dead?"

Methen sat back. "A group of them showed up in Ren. Rada," he said meaningfully. "They burned the local garrison while the men inside slept. There were a couple hundred men in there. Only, it didn't go as they had planned. The doors had been barred and barricaded from the outside, but the men inside had some secret way out that no one knew about. There was a battle in the streets. Meanwhile," he said with a big breath, "the fire from the garrison spread to the warehouses and the dock, and that all went up in flames too. Half the town was in flames all along the waterfront."

"No more of those good dates from Spergia, looks like," said Father. He had really liked those, Jad remembered, though perhaps more for the good price he had gotten and not their bitterness.

"Not for a while, no," said Methen. None of the smiles he'd given for Father trying to be jokeful reached his eyes. "Especially as that's when the army came back."

"Army?" asked Father.

"The Rada we had here was telling the truth. A thousand men escorting one bride, betrothed to the master of the horse lords."

"She must be some woman," said Father.

"The merchants said that the masters of Ren had already sent out a delegation to meet them, to let them know what had happened. They didn't want them to think it was some sort of revolt against the Phentinites. Having a garrison, it's good for business, and having an army of a thousand armed soldiers think you killed two hundred of their men ... not so good for business. So they wanted to get ahead of the rumors..."

"Rumors?" Father asked, as he was supposed.

"That the men of their garrison had been killed by a much smaller force, only a few Rada."

"To be expected, in the middle of the night, sleeping only in their modesty?"

Methen shook his head. "Not like this. It was said to be only a few men against nearly two hundred. They didn't know what to think of it. There had been no fighting since, no looting, no demands. It had to be some band of rebels, they thought, trying to get them in trouble with the empire."

"We know better," breathed Father. "Is that what you're trying to say, Methen?"

"We do," said Methen. "The army ... it was met by a man outside the city..."

"The merchants?"

"The army ... on the way back with the merchants ... they were met by a man wearing Rada armor. Skinny, brash ... you know. He only had a few handfuls of men with him, blocking the road. Some of them, the merchants swore, were men they had seen in the town among the garrison just the day before. The man said he had come down from over the mountains to eat the Phentinite Empire ... its armies, the emperor, their god—they laughed at him of course. They thought him a madman. The Phentinite governor ... he had come with the army to bring the girl to be wed ... ordered the army to march on, and their camp set up outside the city. And ... they didn't make it."

"They're dead now," said Mother.

"Not all of them," amended Methen. "The merchants said the soldiers who were sent to arrest the man were killed. So more came, and they too didn't come back. It wasn't a large army, only a thousand men. They were all looking on."

"And they're dead," said Mother.

"The Phentinite governor, yes," said Methen. "Nothing could stop the man who was blocking the way. Spears, swords, nothing. They speared him, burned him—you know, Jobus, you know we've seen it. They told me one of the army's champions chopped his arm off and the man picked up his dropped arm, pried the sword from his own severed hand, and he kept coming. Those who stayed to face him died—scores of them, dead heaps along the river's edge. They say it ran red out to the lake," added Methen like an afterthought he found interesting. "Some of them, they ran away. Another bunch killed the governor—his own guard turned on him, I heard. The rest went with him. Either way, now there's no Phentinite army in Ren anymore. They're gone."

"By Zua..."

"Yes ... no more good dates," said Mother, pointedly.

Jad saw Father look at him, just briefly, and in his eyes Jad saw a flicker of all the nightmares he'd been having for days now, soldiers dying by his hand, scores of them, screaming for their mothers, their wives, for mercy...

"The man ... they said he called himself the Lion..."

THE END

Check out *The Lion*'s bookend in the Speaker Series

THE LAST SPEAKER

**The man out of time. The foreman who takes him in.
The widow who makes the harvest a home.
The six drifters who repay her in magic.**

When the world was young, Joe was advisor to emperors, could challenge gods—he even succeeded in cheating death. Now Joe is the last speaker of magic.

Or so he believes.

Penniless, and hopping a train, he meets three hoboes who don't just show him the ropes of riding the rails. They show him magic hasn't faded out of the world the way he thought...

Working as a farm laborer with them, and keeping his own abilities secret, it feels like he's found his people again, and for the first time in eons he's shocked to discover he has something to lose.

Unfortunately, as Joe knows so well, very little lasts forever. Now, if he can't help hold his newfound friends together, he'll have to show them what he can do to make their remaining time unforgettable.

Acknowledgements

It takes a village to raise a book—even if it's to point out its deep flaws and give a hearty chuckle. In this case, I need to give special thanks to my lifelong alpha reader, Michael Burton—having one fan is often enough. Special thanks to my cover designer, Youness Elh, who nailed what I wanted immediately; my beta reader and fellow historical fantasy author Christopher Matson, who went above and beyond and called up a guy he knew with a freakin' sheep farm for fact checking; my proofers, Reid Minnich and Claire Golden, who gave me the immense satisfaction of pointing out flubs I simply could not see on my own; my intern, Hazel, for not giving me too many discouraging looks when I'd mutter out loud while writing and disturb her naps; and of course to my missus for putting up with me scribbling messy notes and leaving them lying around everywhere, as well as her website prettifying, her font advice, graphical tips, book recommendations, market research, and sometimes golden toast and the occasional perfect cup of tea.

All your input was immensely helpful and greatly appreciated.

ABOUT THE AUTHOR

In 2011, Lee Burton won the Percy Janes First Novel Award in the Newfoundland and Labrador Arts and Letters Competition, and in 2017 was a finalist in The Writers of the Future contest. In 2023, he'll be publishing the first of his Speaker Series stories.

Lee Burton lives in St. John's, Newfoundland, where for the past ten years he has worked as a freelance editor with Ocean's Edge Editing, collaborating with numerous bestselling authors from across all genres of fiction. Though his stories are diverse, they all revel in the music and harmony of words, and celebrate imagination.